WINGS & SCYTHE

CW00493314

WINGS & SCYTHE
Copyright © 2024 by Ella Cutich

All rights reserved. No part of this book may be used or reproduced in any matter whatsoever without written permission except in the case of brief quotations embodied in critical articles or reviews.

This is a work of fiction. Names, characters, places, and incidents either are the product of the author's imagination or are used fictitiously. Any resemblance to actual persons, living or dead, events, or locales is entirely coincidental.

Cover design and internal art by Ella Cutich

Cover design images from Shutterstock:
 Wings from SCOTTCHAN/Shutterstock.com
 Scythe from Peyker/Shutterstock.com
 Feathers from Siwakorn1933/Shutterstock.com
 Fantasy text from Didik12/Shutterstock.com

Dedicated to all those who are a little odd.

Chapter 1

It was a long way down. Just standing at this altitude made Dante feel woozy. *No wonder they choose this place to die.*

He stood on one of the towers of the Golden Gate Bridge. The wind threatened to blow him right off the tower, but his scythe's weight anchored him. Down below, the water was not liquid at all but a solid surface. Hitting the water from this high up would be instant death.

His eyes focused on a boy far below him on the bridge. Jumping down from the top of the tower, he landed on the walking path.

"Don't do it." Dante knew Alex couldn't hear him. But Dante wished it so much that it manifested into words.

Gripping the railing, Alex bent his knees. He paused long enough for Dante to think he might change his mind, but no. Instead, Alex thrusted his middle finger to the sky and leaped off the bridge. He held up his vulgar sign all the way down. It was like he was dying out of spite.

He smacked the water with a sickening splat. His body sank beneath the murky depths. But not his soul. It levitated above the water, glowing with an ethereal light.

Dante jumped after him, slowing to hover over the water. His black robe grazed the surface.

"I'm not dead?" Alex asked, annoyed.

Dante swung his scythe, severing the link between Alex's soul and body.

"Now you are," Dante said.

"Good!" Alex declared. He looked back at some place back on shore, toward the city. "I never have to deal with any of that crap again. It's over. It's finally over." His voice cracked as he repeated the phrase.

Dante shook his head. "It's only begun."

***

Dante sliced the air in a wide arc with his scythe. A tear appeared in the sky like a wound. It shimmered and stretched until it was as tall as him.

"Let's go," Dante said.

Alex wiped away the tears in his eyes. "Do I have to?"

Dante shrugged. "I'm not going to force you. But if you don't, then your soul will fade, a ghost of its former self, doomed to haunt this spot until the end of time."

Alex scowled. "*Sheesh.* I was going to anyway."

And with that, Alex stepped through the tear with Dante right behind. It was quick and painless, but Dante always closed his eyes, afraid of what he might see and never would unsee.

His feet stepped on crumbling ground, rising to a dusty hill. The tear shrunk and disappeared. All around them were scraggly shrubs and stubborn weeds growing in the cracks of dirt. Overhead, gray clouds lined the sky, blocking out the sun. A gloomy mist surrounded them.

"This is Purgatory," Dante said, returning his scythe to his harness on his back.

"I have to say, I'm unimpressed."

Dante had to smile. *He's really taking this in stride.* His eyes flickered toward the huge balance scale up the hill. The corners of his mouth dropped. *The death part was easy. This is where it truly begins.*

At the top of the hill, a huge balance scale shone from an internal light. Its brass gleamed as if it was freshly polished. Two huge weighing pans on either side were held up by chains that were connected to the beam.

Alex's eyes widened. "They never talked about this in Sunday School."

Dante shrugged, trying to be casual, but his chest was tight with nerves. He had no idea how to even begin to explain. He just wanted this part to be over.

"I'm going to go see," Alex said. He marched right toward it.

In one quick motion, Dante removed his scythe from his back and swung. The curved blade caught Alex by the waist, stopping him in his tracks.

"What're you doing?"

Dante tugged his scythe's handle, pulling Alex back in the crook of his blade. "We have to wait our turn." His eyes followed the line of reapers and their accompanying souls up the hill to the balance scale.

"Seriously? What are we waiting for?" Alex crossed his arms.

A tap on his shoulder made Dante jump. A reaper appeared at his side with his assignment in tow. "Hey, I know this is your first real job. Seems like this human is giving you trouble." The reaper glanced at Alex, who scowled. "Let me know if you need help."

Dante gulped, wishing the ground would swallow him up. It was true this was his first assignment, but he had been tagging along with his parents for years.

"Thanks, but I got this," Dante said.

The reaper gave him a look. Dante knew that look all too well. *He thinks I don't know what I'm doing.*

"Are you sure?" The reaper stared hard as if boring the question into him.

Dante gritted his teeth. "I'm sure."

"Are you going to move forward? I've got a schedule to keep." Another reaper griped at him from behind.

Dante looked in front of him to see a gap in the line. "Oh, right." He stepped forward, making sure Alex followed. His jaw clenched. He willed himself to keep his face neutral but it burned anyway.

"Wow, you're turning red. You really *are* new at this," Alex commented. Too loud, in Dante's opinion.

Dante glared at him. *How quickly I went from feeling sorry for him to being annoyed.*

"Okay, look, I'll be a good boy and wait in line." Alex held up his hands. "I wouldn't want to embarrass you in front of your reaper friends."

Someone stifled a laugh behind him.

Then stop talking. Dante held his tongue, but his thoughts boiled.

A scream interrupted all conversations. "Please, no! Not Hell!" Then no more words were heard, only screams until heavy silence permeated the air.

Dread cooled down Dante's temper. *Soon enough, it will be our turn.* He side-eyed Alex, waiting for more comments, but the screams seemed to shut him up, too. Dante returned his scythe to his harness once more. Hopefully, he wouldn't need it again.

Reapers and their assignments shuffled forward. A new space in the line formed, but this time, Dante closed the gap right away. In the tense quietness, a melodic voice rang out from the top of the hill.

"What's that guy saying?" Alex craned his neck.

The last time Dante didn't answer him, it only made more trouble. *Let's not repeat that.*

"He's doing the judgment of the soul," Dante said.

"What? I thought that was God's job."

"That's for the Final Judgment." Dante mentally crossed his fingers because he didn't know how to explain it any further.

Alex opened his mouth, but luckily—only for Dante—he was saved by more screams. Another voice, female this time, pleaded for mercy. The wails intensified. Dante imagined the woman was at the gate of Hell, her fingers grasping at anything that would delay the nightmare even for a fraction of a second.

And then the screams stopped. Everyone stepped forward.

"This is depressing," Alex said.

"Yes." *For once, we agree on something.*

Alex side-eyed Dante. "So this is like your job? You get paid?"

"Paid? No. It's my duty to be a reaper."

"So, you didn't choose this?"

"No, God created me for this purpose."

Alex thought for a moment. "What was my purpose? My life sucked. How did that help anything?"

Again, Dante didn't know how to answer that. But a pang of sympathy came back. *I shouldn't be annoyed at him. He doesn't understand anything going on. Not that I know much more.*

Screams and shuffling. There was a rhythm to it—horrific as it was. As they drew closer, the voice on the hill rang clearer and words were more pronounced.

Alex leaned in to hear. "So this guy says the same thing every time?"

Dante nodded. "Yes, I've heard it so many times. It gets tiring."

"I'm tired of it already."

Dante chuckled, despite himself. "You have no idea."

He glanced over at Alex and they shared a grin.

More screams and shuffling. Now they were at the top of the rocky hill. The mist drew back from the giant balance scale. From up close, it shined even brighter like a beacon. The weight was evenly distributed between the two pans despite a white feather laying on the right one. The other was empty—for now.

An angel stepped into view. His wings were tucked in, but the tops of his wings peeked over his shoulders. His long white robe rippled as he glided over to the boy. The angel had perfectly cropped tawny hair and marble skin that was only marred by the grimace on his chiseled face.

"Alex Miller," Gabriel announced, invoking him forward. Gabriel did not address Dante or even look his way. Like all reapers, he was invisible to angels until they were needed.

"Your soul is to be judged against the Feather of Truth. If your heart weighs the same as the Feather, then you may pass through the gates of Heaven." Here, Gabriel waved an elegant arm toward his right. Further back, the golden gate gleamed but remained firmly shut.

Through the gaps in the bars, Dante saw a glow, nothing else. He didn't know what lay beyond. Heaven's Gate stayed closed for him, too.

The angel waved his left arm, gesturing toward the opposite way. "If your heart is heavier than the Feather, you will go—"

"Yeah, yeah, I've heard it before," Alex interrupted, yawning. "Can we get this over with?"

Gabriel shot a horrified look at Dante. "Control your assignment!"

Dante shrugged. "He's right. Everyone knows there's only two options. I think we can figure out the other one." He crossed his arms as if in defiance but it was really just to calm his pounding heart. He hated this part.

"This is protocol, Dante," he admonished. "I thought your elders would have taught you that."

Dante's frown deepened. "Whatever, you like lording over humans."

Gabriel lifted his chin. "I will let The Council know how you address an angel."

Dante clenched his teeth, knowing he screwed up already. *My first real assignment and I'm already getting a talking-to.*

"Hey, so you gonna judge my heart or what?" Alex asked, cocking his head to the side.

Alex seemed so calm about this. *Does he already know which gate will be swinging open?*

"You make us look unbecoming, Dante," Gabriel censured him before resuming his theatrical prose.

"I will now take your heart and place it on the scale. And I will then weigh your heart, which embodies all your good deeds and sins. Thusly—"

"Oh man, looks like I'm going to the furnace." Alex shrugged and then grinned at Dante.

Dante was taken aback. "You're okay with that?"

"I don't want to go to Heaven anyway," Alex said, stunning both of them. "It sounds boring. What would I do there anyway? Just sit around on clouds all day? No thanks."

Gabriel's face contorted in ways Dante had never seen before. The closest was when Dante snuck a chicken feather on the scale to see if it weighed the same as the angelic one. It didn't and he was grounded for a month.

Dante laughed at Gabriel's lack of composure and Alex flashed another grin. They were like comrades in arms. Finally, someone else who was done with all this crap.

Gabriel went crimson as he stomped over to Alex. Without another word, he yanked out Alex's heart. Alex gasped as he fell to the ground. He clutched his chest, doubling over in pain.

The angel threw the beating heart into the weighing pan. The whole scale wobbled up and down. For a moment, it evened out, but then it quickly dropped like the heart was made of stone.

"You know what to do," Gabriel snapped, now completely done with all his pretense. "And you will regret this transgression, I promise this!"

Dante groaned, knowing full well he would, but for now, he would relish the moment. It was nice to see an angel get knocked down a peg.

He pulled Alex up as he continued to gasp for breath.

"Okay, let's do this." Alex's eyes shone with determination. Dante had never seen anyone so eager to go to Hell. All Dante knew of that place was the screaming. Everyone always screamed as they passed through the gates.

"Alright then," Dante said. At least Alex was making this part easier for him. His father had to literally pull humans off of him and throw them inside the gates. His mother reprimanded him for it, but what else was there to do? He was glad it wouldn't happen this time—he was already in enough trouble.

Dante opened Hell's gate, which groaned from too much use.

Alex peered in, not yet crossing the boundary. From here, they couldn't see much except the color red.

"Thanks, man," Alex said, turning back to Dante.

"You're thanking me?"

Alex cocked his head to the side. "Yeah, I got to have a cool reaper for my death."

"If you say so, but aren't you scared to go to Hell?"

"It will most likely suck," he admitted. "But after what I did, I'm not surprised. I deserve it."

Dante shook his head. He didn't understand how Alex was so candid about all this.

"Well, goodbye," Dante said. He felt a twinge of sadness as he realized he would never see Alex again.

Alex raised his hand in a peace sign as he crossed the border into Hell. Quickly, Dante shut the gate, not wanting to hear him scream like everyone else did. Dante wanted to go on believing that somehow, Alex could even shrug off Hell.

Chapter 2

Dante stood before The Council. So Gabriel did tell on him. *I knew it.*

All the angels had a matching scowl on their faces as they lined up in front of Dante. They stood with their arms crossed. For a moment, everyone was silent, even though their faces said enough. To distract himself, Dante glanced around, trying to pretend he didn't feel their deadly gazes piercing him.

It was a huge, rounded chamber with the ceiling extending high into the stratosphere, purposely making Dante feel small and insignificant. Gold swirls and crosses decorated the marble walls, and larger-than-life statues lined the walls, depicting various Biblical scenes. The one closest to him was from the Old Testament where the angel was diving down from Heaven to stop Abraham from sacrificing his son. Dante focused on the angel. Was that when angels actually cared about humans? Because it seemed like they didn't anymore.

The angel in the center stepped forward. She had a matching white robe like the rest of them, but hers had been adorned with an additional golden garment, so everyone would know how special she was. When she spoke, she made sure her words reverberated throughout the chamber.

"You have been charged with contempt and obstruction to the protocol in addition to the way you inappropriately addressed an angel." She glowered at him, making her disapproval quite clear.

Dante tried to keep his face as neutral as possible.

"Do you accept these charges?" she asked.

Her dark, glossy hair reflected the light, creating a circle at the top of her head. Dante supposed that was where humans got the idea that angels had halos. But what humans didn't realize was angels had a stick up their—

"Dante, please respond," his mother whispered. The *please* was as much as a formality as this whole trial. It didn't matter if he agreed or not, these charges weren't going away and whatever the consequence was, he wasn't going to like it.

"Yes," Dante said, and when he saw the angel frown, he added, "Ma'am."

The angel peered at him over her spectacles. "I understand that this was your first assignment. The Council has agreed to show mercy"—Dante stifled a laugh—"and will offer you to only take silver cases for ten years."

Dante felt his mouth open in protest before he could stop himself. His mother saw and quickly jabbed him in the side. It hurt, but it hurt less than any punishment the angels could bestow upon him. He sighed internally instead. Silver cases were the nice term for only reaping the elderly. It was boring work because most of them died in retirement homes.

"Do you agree to this punishment?"

Again, this was another annoying formality.

"Yes, ma'am," Dante said. He knew this really was better than he thought.

The angel wasn't done yet. She said, "I expect that you do not conflate our mercy with weakness and try any other transgressions." She gave Dante a hard look. "Next time, there will be no mercy."

It sounded weak, but Dante believed her. He didn't know what the threat entailed, but he knew he had already crossed the line. No more cool places to visit, like the Golden Gate Bridge.

His mother and father bowed respectfully, and he followed suit with clenched fists. He hated having to lower himself to angels. Why were they so special?

***

Back at home, they hung their scythes on the wall by the door. His father's handle was worn from use, but the oak was still strong. The blade had some dings in it from all the times souls were trying to escape and he swung and missed. His mother's blade shone like a mirror, and her handle was carefully polished. Dante's was a beginner's scythe before he could earn his "real" one—whatever that meant.

The home itself was simple. Rough wooden boards lined the walls and floor as well as the ceiling. It looked as if they were living in a box. As soon as Dante entered, he felt the walls closing in.

The wood had aged some and certain planks had twisted and shrunk, leaving gaps for cold air to sneak in. The small, brick fireplace tried its best to fight off the chill even as its flames shuttered against it.

They sat down for dinner at the cramped table. His mother spread out the meal in front of them—their portioned meal of watery soup and stale bread, along with a jug of murky water.

His mother sat without eating anything. Instead, she fixed her bun, twirling her hair and securing it back. She smoothed her hair, making sure all the little wisps of hair were in place.

His father ate his dinner with his eyes focused on the plate and nothing else.

Dante sat, feeling suffocated by the silence. They didn't need to say anything. Their thoughts were screaming at him. His gumption from earlier leaked away as he realized he had made things harder for them, too. They didn't have a direct consequence like he did, but he knew his actions reflected poorly on them as parents. The angels judged them, maybe even more than him.

Dante took a bite of bread and instantly regretted it. The bread sucked out all the saliva from his mouth and caught in his throat like a stone. Coughing, he gulped down some gross water to add moisture to it. He swallowed the bread, feeling the hard lump slide down into his chest. He threw the rest of the bread down on the table.

He stood up. "I'm done eating."

"No, you're not," his father snapped.

"I'm not hungry," Dante said.

"You will sit down and finish your dinner!"

"Why?" Dante asked, his voice rising.

His father slammed his fists on the table, rattling the dishes. "Because I said so!"

"I said I'm not hungry," Dante repeated, digging in his heels.

"Could you listen to us for once?" his mother asked, her eyes woeful.

Dante swallowed as he looked at them both. Despite his father's angry outburst, he only looked exhausted. His mother's eyes watered as she silently pleaded with him. Dante knew he was hurting them even more, but he couldn't help himself. His veins burned with fire.

"I'm tired of all of this!" Dante said. "I'm tired of stale bread and gross water. I'm tired of the stupid angels thinking they're better than us. I'm tired of having to listen to everyone else and do what everyone else wants me to do. I'm tired of sending people to Hell—I don't want to do that for the rest of my life!" His heart felt like it was going to burst into flames.

"Calm down," his mother said as she brushed back a hair that had fallen. *Of course,* Dante silently raged. *Everything has to be in its place.* His mother didn't really care about him. She just wanted him to stay in his place, too.

"No." He slammed the door on his way out.

"Get back here!" his father shouted.

Dante plugged his ears.

***

Dante climbed the rocky hill to his high spot, overlooking the town. An eerie glow cast through the streets. Rows of identical, small houses lined the streets in a perfect grid. One road led out of the town, winding up another hill in the distance. At the top of the far hill was the town hall. With its tall, pitched roof, it looked like a black arrow silhouetted against the light. Seeing the town hall made him frown as he recalled his punishment. *Silver cases for the next ten years. Just great.*

Sighing, he shifted his position back to the moon where it loomed over the horizon, gleaming in the clear gray sky. Its phases matched those of Earth's moon, which was odd. Purgatory wasn't out there in space, but on a plane of its own, where humans couldn't pass until they died. But somehow, the places were connected.

He focused on the stars. And somewhere, on another plane, was Heaven. He had never been there. Apparently, once upon a time, angels and reapers both lived in Heaven, but angels didn't like that reapers were in contact with sinners. They thought reapers were soiling their precious place. Reaping souls made them unclean, unfit to be in Heaven, so the angels forced them to move to Purgatory.

His father's words echoed in his head. "And that's why angels don't like us. We are beneath them, tainted with sin."

Dante looked at his hands. *Am I really tainted with sin? I have no idea. How could sin be contagious? It's not a disease,* he reasoned. *It is a choice to sin.*

He sighed as he scanned the sleepy reaper town. He wished he could talk to Tommy. But he was sure everyone had heard what he did, so anyone seeing him out past curfew would tell his parents and get him into more trouble.

The wind softly carried the scent of chrysanthemums in the cool air. Goosebumps pricked his skin. The sun had been down for a while and with it went the warmth. It was getting late and tomorrow was going to be another annoying day.

In a huff, he begrudgingly went home.

Chapter 3

The gloomy silence persisted through the morning as Dante trudged to the town hall with his father and mother. Many other reapers swarmed out of the other identical houses. All of them were adorned in black robes, long scythes, and huge yawns.

The bell tolled—an angry reminder to anyone who wasn't on their way to the town hall to hurry up. *Death Knell*, they called it. Another day, another death. It seemed like someone was always dying.

Bright red hair appeared in the crowd of black robes.

"Hey, Tommy," he said, trying to sound off-hand, like he didn't just get himself into a load of trouble.

Tommy threw him back a wicked grin.

"I probably shouldn't talk to you," he teased. "I heard you were in front of The Council."

Frowning, Dante figured everyone would have something to say about that.

"I'm kidding." Tommy punched his arm. He gave Dante another smile, this time more reassuring.

Dante shrugged, forcing himself to grin despite his gloom. "No worries."

"So what's your punishment?" Tommy asked, lowering his voice among the other reapers, but they were leaning in to hear anyway.

Keeping his voice casual, Dante replied, "Just silver cases for a decade."

Tommy's eyebrows raised, losing themselves in his mop of red hair. "That sucks."

They reached the town hall, a wooden building with a bell on top. It rang again. Its chime clanged right above him. The clashing metal vibrated in his ears. Dante resisted the urge to cover them, pretending like it didn't bother him.

"What about you?" he asked after the bell finished ringing.

"I'm taking red cases now," Tommy said. He tried to say it nonchalantly, but his green eyes sparkled with excitement.

Dante was impressed. Red cases were for murder victims. It was horrible for the victim, but it made for cool stories to tell to other reapers. Everyone loved horror stories, but only when it happened to someone else.

They entered the town hall and got into line. Too soon it was Dante's turn at the counter. He sighed a long, heavy sigh as he received the page of silver cases.

The receptionist glared at him. "It's not my fault you can't hold your tongue."

He grimaced. It always amazed him how fast information traveled. But this time, he did hold his tongue.

Glancing at the list, he had quite a full load. Another reason why these cases sucked. Not many reapers wanted these jobs, so for the unlucky few, they were overloaded.

Tommy pulled him over to the side. Looking up, Dante realized he was still in the way of the others waiting for their lists.

"Staring at it won't make it any better," Tommy said. "Come on, let's get breakfast."

Nodding, Dante folded the paper and scrunched it inside his inner pocket of his robe. They pushed past other people. The town hall was really one big area, but as soon as they all piled into it, the room seemed way too small.

They made their way to the far side of the room where loaves of bread were stacked on a few wooden tables.

The only good thing about breakfast was the bread was the freshest at the beginning of the day. Dante took a loaf and wrapped it in a cloth, although he didn't know why. He still got crumbs on his robe and it still turned stale by dinnertime anyway. Memories of his mother carefully wrapping her bread every morning surfaced in his mind. *Everything I do is a culmination of what everyone else does.*

Taking their bread, they pushed out of the town hall. A group of reapers spilled back out onto the dusty road. Since they were early—the next bell hadn't rung yet—they had some more time to eat before their day truly began.

Tommy caught sight of his other friends. With a reassuring nod from Dante, Tommy left to chat with them. Dante was alright being left alone. He needed some time to think.

A few cypress trees stubbornly grew next to the building. They were skinny, tall, pointy, and didn't offer much shade. The sun began its journey across the sky, and the heat was palpable. He still chose to endure it so he could be away from the crowd.

After taking a few bites, Dante wrapped up the rest of the loaf. He wasn't hungry and was eager to start—just to get it over with.

He pulled out his list. It was made on thick parchment paper, penned in scribbled ink. It was the long list of people who were about to die.

A surreal moment came over him. He wondered what they would think if they knew their time was almost up. Dante shook his head. *Do reapers' names ever show up on here? I couldn't imagine mine appearing one day.*

Reapers did eventually pass on, unable to fulfill their duties. One elderly reaper, Irene, was here one day and gone the next. Even though he was little, he remembered how she would sneak him a cookie, giving it with a wink and one calloused finger on her lips. He never knew where she got them, but she would often give them to kids whenever she could. And when she hadn't been around for a while, he asked his parents where she was.

They just told him to hush and not to talk about her.

We deal with death all the time, eager to swap stories about humans, but when death comes knocking too close to home, everyone gets tight-lipped. I suppose one day, people will hush at my name, until I too am gone from memory.

The Death Knell clanged. The harsh sound reverberated through his bones.

He put away his list—it was time to harvest souls.

Chapter 4

The retirement home was beautiful. It had polished floors, big windows with sun pouring in, and huge sitting areas lined with couches. But the vases were full of fake flowers, the lights were fluorescent and harsh, and everywhere smelled strongly of lemon cleaner—to mask the stench of death.

Dante knew he would see a lot of retirement homes. *More like reaper homes*, he thought grimly. *I'll be here so much, I might as well move in.*

He passed by wrinkly people wobbling on canes or scooting in wheelchairs. Canes and wheels squeaked on the floor, but his boots were silent. No one could see or hear him pass by, but a few could sense his presence as they glanced his way.

In one of the many rows of doors, Dante entered. An old woman laid in bed, propped up by pillows. An opened book was sprawled across her lap, the pages fanning out.

She appeared to be sleeping.

"Lydia Armstrong?" he asked, trying to evoke her soul.

"Yes?" Her soul appeared, slightly transparent and stood next to her slumped body. One strand still connected her to her physical form like an umbilical cord.

"You didn't get to finish reading," he said.

She stared at him. He waited for the questions to start rolling in.

"Oh, honey, I've read it too many times to count."

He shuffled, not expecting that answer. *I hope she doesn't think I'm a visitor.*

He cleared his throat. "You do know you're dead, right?"

She waved his question away. "Of course! I've been ready to die for a while now."

"Is that so?"

She didn't respond, but just looked like she was waiting for him to do something.

So, without another word, he took his scythe off his back. In one smooth motion, he cut the string that connected her soul to her body.

She floated, rising to the ceiling. She looked back down at her slumped physical body and smiled. *Smiled?*

Dante shook his head. "Are you happy to be dead?"

"I was trapped and now I'm free!" She laughed, put her hands up, and twirled around mid-air.

"You don't get it," she said as she spun back around to face Dante. "I couldn't walk. I was stuck in bed all day."

"I'm sure they put you in a wheelchair—"

"Oh, that's not walking. I want to move on my own. To dance like I did when I was young."

And to fulfill her wish, she did so right there in the air, spinning and twirling, with a practiced grace. Once upon a time, she was a ballerina. And for one moment, she was again.

He watched her, slack-jawed. *Who is this woman that is so full of life even death can't stop her?*

But they couldn't be here all day. He had other souls to reap. And this assignment wasn't over yet.

He cleared his throat. "We have to go now," he said reluctantly.

She let her arms fall to her sides. "Alright."

And with that, he led her to her judgment.

***

Dante wished she was still dancing and twirling in the air. He wished to see her smile that brightened up her whole face. To see the strain of her physical body melting away. To see the joy she felt.

It was all gone.

"I'm sorry," he choked.

"Honey, don't worry about it." She patted his hand.

Is she really comforting me right now?

"How are you okay with this?"

"Oh, I wasn't a nice person. I was so bitter when I got in a car accident and could never dance again. I took it out on everyone. I knew it wasn't right, but I was so bitter, so angry." She sighed like she was finally letting go of all that anger.

"All I ever wanted was to dance again." She looked at him, eyes shining. "Thank you. You let me dance one more time. I am truly grateful for it."

She squeezed his hand but it felt like she was squeezing his heart. He didn't want her to go to Hell. It didn't seem right.

"Dante," Gabriel warned. His perfect porcelain face fractured as his lips cracked into a frown. "It is time."

Dante sighed. *Do angels even have feelings? It's like they are immune.*

But he did have Lydia's permission. It felt slightly better that she was at least willing to go through with this.

He opened the iron gate. The crimson hue spilled like blood.

Without another word, she walked to the gate with her head held high.

She was so calm, but as soon as she crossed the threshold, she screamed. It was a despairing sound that wretched his very soul.

The gate closed, snapping shut like nothing happened. Like she never existed.

But he could still hear the screams.

Chapter 5

Dante sighed as his next assignment, George Tannenbaum, had his heart weighed on the scale. Gabriel glanced at him, daring him to speak.

He would love to get me into more trouble, Dante thought as he sighed again.

Dante promised himself he wouldn't say anything. But sighing wasn't actually saying anything. He couldn't get into trouble for sighing, could he?

The heart on the scale sank and so did Dante's. *Not another one.*

"You are hereby sentenced to Hell," Gabriel announced.

The man crumbled in a heap. "Oh God, forgive me." He covered his eyes.

Seeing the man so dejected only made this part harder for Dante. He really hoped he wouldn't have to drag him to the gate.

"We gotta go," Dante said as gently as he could. In the corner of his eye, he saw a line of reapers with their assignments waiting for their judgment.

The man nodded—not in agreement but in acceptance of his fate.

George sucked in his breath, but he didn't hesitate as he crossed over the threshold. The red glow consumed him.

Dante shut the gate, but not before he heard him scream.

They always screamed.

***

Dante stood on top of the Golden Gate Bridge. The list of names fluttered in his hand as the wind whipped by. He had many more names to cross off before the day was done, but he couldn't make himself go. Instead, he studied his scythe in his hands as if it held answers.

A memory flashed before his eyes. His hands shook as he took his scythe for the first time. The handle was wooden, only lightly sanded. As he changed his grip, the coarse surface scraped against his skin. The blade's edge was rough and unrefined. The other reapers' scythes didn't look like this. When reapers received their first scythes, they were the shiniest and smoothest they would ever be. Even in the moment, he knew something was off.

"This is your beginner's scythe," the old reaper said as if that explained everything. "When you are ready, you receive your real one."

Dante remembered the old reaper's eyes the most. The rest of the man blurred in his memories, but his eyes were as clear as if he was actually looking at him. His wrinkles were so pronounced that they created valleys of shadows around his eyes. The whites of his eyes yellowed with age, but it did not diminish the piercing, intelligent blue of his irises.

Even in his memory, Dante felt the strong urge to ask what the old man meant. But he was the eldest reaper who initiated the new recruits so he didn't inquire. That was when he was younger. When he was a good boy and didn't ask questions.

Dante did mention it to his mother. He remembered how his mother scrunched her eyes and pursed her lips. It seemed like she also wanted to ask questions but she closed her face off from forming those thoughts.

He placed his scythe in its harness. He didn't want to look at it anymore, but now he felt the weight of it on his back. *I don't want a new scythe, my real scythe, or any other scythe. I don't want to deal with any of this anymore.*

Alex went to Hell. Lydia went to Hell. George went to Hell. How many more humans will I have to send?

The logical part of him knew they went to Hell for a reason. They made bad choices. They chose their path.

But this Father Almighty, all-seeing, all-knowing, ever-loving God created a world of suffering and free will. *Why give humans free will then punish them when they choose wrong? It's a set up for failure.*

Do they truly have to suffer for eternity when their lives are so minuscule compared to the infinity of time? Why do any of this? Why does any of this matter?

Dante's head swarmed with doubts. Questions stung at him. They left no answers, only painful thoughts. *I'm a spoke of the wheel, this endless cycle of reaping souls and sending them to their doom. I'm a part of this corrupt system.*

A seagull squawked next to him as it flew past, inches away from him. For a moment, his thoughts were interrupted, and he watched the bird soar in the sky.

The bird flew on the wind. Its wings were outstretched, with nothing but sky above and water underneath. It was free. Free from any worries. Free from sin.

Free.

He let go of his list.

It too was carried by the wind, sharing the sky with the seagull.

***

The Death Knell tolled. It was another day. Dante laid in his lumpy bed, even though he had been wide awake for a while now. The haze of dawn spread across the horizon and into his room. He stared at the water stains in the ceiling, not wanting to get up.

He didn't reap any souls yesterday.

And he wasn't going to today either.

He decided he would still take the list from the town hall like normal. He was sure the list would be even longer this time. But then he would do whatever he wanted to do. Not doing what everyone else wanted him to do.

But he didn't forget about The Council. They warned him to not disobey them again.

And here he was. Not doing what he was supposed to do. Again.

He had no idea what the consequences were for not reaping souls. But it didn't matter. He couldn't do it anymore. He couldn't keep sending humans to Hell. Whether they deserved it or not, he didn't care. *I'm done being a part of this system.*

"Dante!" His mother knocked on his door. "You need to get up."

"Okay." He slumped up in his bed. They still had no idea about his decision or his actions from the previous day. How much longer could this go on?

***

He joined the silent march up the hill. Right on time, the Death Knell tolled. Its reverberations carried a haunting tone, a warning in its harsh sound. Like it knew what Dante was doing.

Dante kept his face as normal as possible, in case it portrayed any of his thoughts running through his mind.

"What's wrong?" Tommy asked as he walked up to him.

Well, so much for that. Dante shrugged, not quite looking him in the eye.

"I didn't quite finish the whole list yesterday," he said, nudging at the truth. "You don't think I'll get in trouble for that, do you?" Tommy was the only one he could ask without getting admonished. But Dante wanted to know how big of a deal it was that he wasn't reaping souls.

Out of the corner of his eyes, Dante saw Tommy frown.

"Uh, those things happen, you know?" Tommy ran a hand through his hair, trying to stay casual but his voice wavered. "Just make sure you get them done today, okay?"

Dante pursed his lips. He was hoping for a better reply than that. If happy-go-lucky Tommy was worried, then he definitely was going to be in trouble.

Oh well. Screw it.

***

Dante stepped forward in line. The receptionist handed him his list. He reached for it, but the woman didn't let go.

Looking up, he locked eyes with her. Her eyes scrunched up with scrutiny.

"You have a lot of souls to harvest today," she said. Her voice was laced with warning.

"Yep, I'm going to be busy," Dante answered. He had made his choice, but for some reason, he didn't want to come out and say it. Maybe he wanted to see how far he could take it.

What happens to a reaper who refuses to reap?

Without another word, he took the paper. Or more accurately, the woman released it. He put it in his inner pocket of his robe and met back up with Tommy to claim his breakfast.

Tommy was already talking with a few other reapers.

"So there he was, knife in hand. And I'm standing there, like welp, I know how this is going to end."

The others chuckled appropriately.

"So where did he stab him?" asked Matt, a reaper with bony features and a thin frame.

Tommy made a stabbing motion at his chest.

"Oh, no, not the chest," another replied. Her bright blue eyes sparkled while she pouted with full lips. Dante knew Maria, but she never acknowledged him.

"Yes." Tommy shook his head theatrically. "The worst place to stab someone. Of course, the knife grazed the ribs. My assignment wasn't dead—not yet anyway."

Everyone knew the beats to the story to prompt it along. Dante stood a step back from the group, hovering in the shadows, not really listening. He felt apart from everyone, like he had set things into motion, even though no one knew his decision but him. But it seemed like everywhere he looked, there were warnings in the air.

What forces am I messing with?

"And Dante here," Tommy turned to him, smiling broadly. "Dante, our troublemaker."

Everyone laughed on cue.

They have no idea. Dante pressed his lips together in some semblance of a smile. Usually, Dante liked when Tommy included him, but today Dante wished he could disappear.

"I've never been in front of The Council before." Maria appraised him with a look. Probably the first time she had ever looked his way.

"Yeah, they were annoying." Dante shrugged. "But whatever."

Tommy laughed and clapped his hand on Dante's shoulder. "Only Dante here could be so nonchalant about *The Council.*" His voice lowered dramatically at the end.

Dante felt the approving glances of the other reapers, but he didn't meet anyone in the eyes.

The Death Knell rang. Its harsh sound drowned out all conversations, for which Dante was grateful.

Everyone started to cross to the human realm. The reapers swiped the air with their scythes. In one sweeping motion, the scythe created a tear. Quickly, the tear opened up and they entered. As soon as they disappeared inside, the tear closed up like it was never there.

Dante hung back for a moment, pretending to take his time eating his bread. As he watched the others go, he felt a pull to follow. How easy would it be to go along, doing what everyone else was doing. What everyone expected him to do.

But then he remembered Alex and Lydia crossing into Hell. The blood red hue. The screams. The iron gate, slamming shut.

Dante was powerless to help any of them. *This stupid system. Why would an ever-loving God allow sin and suffering? He didn't have to make it this way.*

Just thinking about it made his blood boil. He wished he could do more, but his only act of rebellion was to refuse to be a part of it. Maybe that was enough.

Chapter 6

Dante wasn't used to all this free time. Usually, the list took most of the day to complete. Reaping souls was busy work. He never had a chance to really do what he wanted, so he took this opportunity to explore. And he had a whole globe of places to see.

He traveled to New York City. He loved the lights, the sounds, the people; every walk of life was there. The place felt alive—a break from all the death. The very ground hummed with energy. The air was filled with the sounds of cars honking, people shouting, and music thudding.

Everyone rushed by as he roamed the packed streets. He didn't bother getting out of the way as people hurried through him, unaware of his presence besides a shudder and an odd look over their shoulders before continuing on.

He breathed a sigh of relief. *A break, finally.*

A bus screeched up ahead. Horns blazed. People screamed. Crunching metal and shattering glass pierced the air.

As Dante drew closer, he saw someone lying on the road. Screams of pain never got any easier to hear. The poor man was pleading for help, but it was too late. He was already dead.

Dante stopped in his tracks. His eyes locked on the soul separating from the body. People were getting out of their cars, calling an ambulance, rushing to help. They were completely unaware it was all for nothing.

Then came the reaper.

At first, it was just a swirl of black robes and an arched blade. But for some reason, the reaper stopped amidst all the sirens and screaming and looked at Dante dead in the eyes. It was skin-and-bone Matt from earlier.

"What are you doing here? This is my assignment." Even though Matt was a stone's throw away, his voice sounded like he was right next to Dante.

"I know, I was on my way to mine," Dante lied.

In the blink of an eye, Matt closed the distance between them.

"I've seen you," Matt said. "You haven't been keeping up on your reaper duties. You have a target on your back and now you are making all reapers look bad."

Dante scowled. "I wasn't trying to."

"I don't care. Angels don't even like us when we keep our heads down and do our jobs. But now they're really cracking down on us."

"What're you talking about?"

Matt nodded to his right. A man was watching them. He looked normal enough—just a man wearing a t-shirt and jeans. But to a reaper's eye, Dante saw a glow about him.

"He's an angel disguised as a human. Ever since your incident, they have been watching all the reapers. You're apparently so thick-headed you didn't notice."

Dante wanted to argue but he had nothing to say.

"Talking to you like this will probably get me in trouble," Matt snapped. "Go reap a soul already!"

With a sigh, Dante reluctantly looked at his list while Matt glared at him and tapped his foot. The list kept getting longer. As the scroll unrolled, brushing the road at his feet, he read the first name. *Sarah Williams, death by natural causes, Happy Home Retirement Center, Wednesday at 6:07 a.m.*

Another retirement home, of course. Dante's eyes flickered back up at Matt. He really didn't want to reap, but he also didn't want Matt to get in trouble. Dante's eyes darted back to the angel in disguise. He stared back at him. *They're definitely watching.*

"Fine," Dante snapped. He didn't like how he was being pressured into something that he didn't want to do.

Matt scowled. It made him appear even more skull-like. "Now go!"
Dante rolled his eyes and grabbed his scythe.

***

Dante barely glanced around. Every retirement home was generic.
Nothing about them was welcoming. *You come here and never leave.
Just waiting to die.*

He entered the room through the door. It was closed but that didn't
stop him. Sunlight poured in from a big window. The sun was so bright
that it made the room feel warm and stuffy. A standard issued bed,
table, and chair were neatly arranged, but everything else was stripped
bare. No pictures, no nick-nacks, and nobody. No one was living here.

Frowning, Dante checked his list again. *It's never wrong.*

"Hello?" The voice sounded like a frail old woman.

Dante glanced around but didn't see anyone.

"Can you hear me?"

He looked up. A frightened old woman floated toward the ceiling.

A pang of regret shot through him. How could he forget that if he
didn't reap, the souls would turn into ghosts? She had died a day ago,
but her soul was still trapped here, not able to move on. What if by not
reaping, he was keeping her from Heaven? Just because he had the bad
luck of getting assignments who went to Hell didn't mean they all did.

"Come with me," he said gently. His only hope now was he would
lead her to the golden gates and not the iron ones.

***

"You are sentenced to Hell," Gabriel announced.

Dante stared at the poor, pitiful woman. "Why? What could she
have possibly done to deserve Hell?" He knew it was a mistake to reap
her soul.

Gabriel gave him a stern look. "Not this again."

"Why should she go to Hell? Can you tell me?"

"Her heart has been weighed against the Feather of Truth!"

"Yeah, and why are we trusting this feather?"

Gabriel turned red with rage. "I will alert the Council at once!"

"Go ahead!"

The gates of Hell rattled.

Dante's eyes widened. The gate never rattled before.

"Let me out!" The voice sounded young and feminine. But more than that, her voice was full of anguish and distress. "Please, I'm innocent!"

How is that possible?

There was such desperation in her voice that his feet moved toward the gate, acting on instinct. He had to help this person, whomever she was.

Gabriel stepped in front of him.

"Stop," he commanded. "We are never allowed to open the gate for anyone banished to Hell."

"But she's innocent," Dante protested. Her voice rang so true, so woeful, he believed her words.

Gabriel humphed. He didn't seem to share the same sentiment. "That's what they all say."

Dante started to open his mouth to protest again but closed it instead. As much as he hated to agree with an angel, Gabriel did have a point. Dante knew no one went to Hell unless they deserved it.

No one could be in Hell and be innocent. Right?

***

The voice called out again, louder and more earnest. He saw something from beyond the gate—a pure white pushing back the blood red. But he couldn't make out more than that.

"I have to send this sinner to Hell," Dante said, trying to keep his voice neutral. It was really an excuse to open the gate.

Gabriel frowned, knowing he spoke the truth. The line of reapers was growing even longer.

"You better not let that sinner out or I'll send you to Hell myself," he warned.

Dante shrugged at the empty threat. *There's no way he could do that.* He led Sarah to the gate, eager to see what lay beyond.

He swung the gate open wide. It groaned as it swiveled.

And there stood an angel.

Dante couldn't fully grasp what he was seeing. He was well aware of what angels looked like. The white wings were a dead giveaway. But in Hell? He had the history lesson about a group of rebel angels who defied God and were sent to Hell as a punishment. But that was a long time ago. And this angel was young, about his age. Her golden hair fell in waves around her delicate features. She was the perfect image of what an angel should be. Except her golden eyes were wide with panic.

She grabbed his arm. "Help me!"

Dante was surprised. No angel had ever asked him for aid. But she was in such despair, he pulled her across the threshold. He had to save her. Gabriel yelled at him from a distance, but Dante ignored him.

But as quickly as she appeared, she was gone—yanked away in the mist of red.

Dante could hardly breathe. He couldn't process what happened. It almost seemed like a dream, except his arm still felt the warmth of her hand.

Who was that? Dante wished he could have opened the gate sooner. Then the girl would have been able to escape. He stood there for another few moments, waiting for something else to happen. It didn't.

Gabriel crossed his arms. "Dante! Such impudence! You are going to The Council at once!"

Dante groaned. *Here we go again.*

Chapter 7

It was déjà vu. Here he was in The Council Room again. Everything was an endless cycle, spinning round and round, never going anywhere.

He faced the row of angels, all scowls and hard eyes.

Like before, his father and mother were at his sides. He sighed internally. He was sure they were tired of being the "bad" parents since their son kept getting into trouble. His father and mother side-eyed each other. They looked worried and perplexed. And there was something else in their faces that he couldn't pinpoint.

A cold stone sunk in his stomach. A faint buzz tingled across his arms and the back of his neck. At first, he wasn't sure what he was feeling. Then he understood the unknown expression on his parents' faces.

It was fear.

An angel stepped forward. The same angel with glasses and long brown hair.

"You have been called in front of The Council again," the angel declared. "After only two days, you have chosen to disobey your orders again." She let that last *again* snap, sending echoes throughout the huge hall. Everything else was dead silent. The anger in the air was palatable.

No mercy, his thoughts echoed. *They might actually mean it, too.* The buzzing on his arms intensified.

"Not only have you not done your duty of reaping souls—which is bad enough—but we have been informed that you attempted to let a sinner escape from Hell."

She paused. The silent hall erupted into frenzy whispers.

"Dante!" his mother hissed. "How could you?"

He didn't answer.

His father bowed his head, ashamed.

"It wasn't a sinner," Dante said, making his voice rise above the others.

All the whispers stopped. Everyone turned toward him.

"Oh?" said the angel, adjusting her glasses.

"She wasn't a sinner," he repeated. He truly believed the angel. He had seen sinners. She didn't carry the burden of sin in her eyes like the others did. "She was innocent. Of course I tried to free her."

The angel pursed her lips at his words. "So you admit it freely."

"That I tried to help an innocent? Yeah, I admit that."

Whispers emerged again.

"There are no innocents in Hell," she said. "Who you tried to help was a fallen angel."

Dante blinked in surprise. So it was true. But she looked his age. And the Falling happened long before his time.

Mutters became more fervent and frenzied. The buzzing on his arms grew stronger and spread throughout his body.

The angel glared over her glasses at everyone, imposing her will upon them. They fell silent instantly.

"And now it is the judgment," she continued. "You have been found guilty of abandoning your reaper duties as well as attempting to allow a sinner to escape. For such crimes, the punishment should be right and just."

Right and just. Dante snorted.

The angel took a breath and straightened her posture.

The buzzing on his arms felt like an army of bees beneath his skin.

"You have disobeyed God and denied your reason for existence. You are hereby sentenced to Hell."

His parents gasped. *No, there's no way they can do that.* His whole world tilted and spun. Never again could he see his parents or hang out with Tommy. His life as he knew it was over forever. It felt like the ground beneath him cracked and gave way, his body falling into the void.

His mother clutched his arm. "Please don't do this," she begged the angels. "Couldn't there be another punishment? He's just a boy."

"He is old enough to understand there are consequences for his actions," the angel said with no trace of emotion in her voice.

His mother sobbed loudly. A jab of guilt punched his stomach.

Murmurs erupted into gasps and screams. Even some of the other angels had a horrified look on their faces. No one had been sentenced to Hell since the Falling.

Dante stood there, blinking. He hardly understood what was happening. Everything moved in slow motion. Voices were muffled. He barely felt his father's arms around him, giving him a hug for the last time.

Then he saw the reapers.

The angels parted, making way for them. These reapers didn't deal with human souls.

They appeared like seven looming shadows. Their hoods covered their heads. Not even their eyes could be seen. Gripping their scythes with bony fingers, they held their weapons in front of them—a synchronized motion that gathered dread in Dante's chest.

They came for him.

Dante gulped but his mouth was dry. The silent shadows surrounded him. They blocked his view of his parents until he could see only darkness. The hall fell into a fearful silence.

The reapers raised their scythes high in the air.

Pushing aside the dread, he let his anger boil to the surface.

"I haven't done anything wrong," he said, lifting his chin. "I will escape Hell."

The scythes dropped to the ground in unison. The clanging sound reverberated in his very being. An opening appeared beneath Dante. As the floor disappeared, the pull of gravity dragged him down.

Fear rose in his throat. His whole body felt like a block of ice.

His head spun as realization kicked in.

He was falling to Hell.
He screamed.

Chapter 8

How long does it take to fall to Hell?

Of all the times Dante had sent souls to this place, it had never occurred to him. Of course, he didn't know they were falling. Everything looked red every time he opened the gate. *That's why they always screamed.*

The air howled in his ears. His hair whipped around and stung his eyes. He reached out, trying to cling onto something but only rushing air filled his hands. To give a sense of time—a sense of order—to the chaos of tumbling, plummeting, and whirling was not possible.

And so he fell.

Words echoed in his head. *You have disobeyed God and denied your reason for existence.* Images appeared in his mind. Black-robed figures crowded his peripheral. Long, curved blades shone in the light. *You are sentenced to Hell.* The ground broke beneath him, opening like a mouth and swallowing him whole. As his feet touched air and gravity yanked him down, the words followed him: *This is right and just.*

No, I am right. His fingers twisted into fists. Why give humans free will then punish them when they choose wrong?

This question was lost in the wind like screams in the void. No one heard. No one cared. He was but a drop in an ocean, one grain of sand upon its beach. Fire burned in his veins. Deep inside of him, he knew the truth—his rebellion meant nothing. *Who am I against the power of God? Nothing.* Fury tightened in his chest. His nails dug into his palms. It made him sick.

And still he fell.

Vague shapes whizzed by. He couldn't make anything out. His eyes strained to latch onto something, anything. His mind spun as much as his body did.

Finally, his eyes focused on a dark spot that slowly came closer and closer.

It was the ground. All he could do was watch in horror as the dark spot spread until it took up his whole field of vision.

Time slowed. The dark ground was comprised of rocks with many pointy, rough edges like a big pile of obsidian daggers. For a moment, he was suspended, hovering in the air and staring face-first at a pointy stone dagger. The point was poised at his left eye. His breath caught in his throat. *Everything I have done and have failed to do has led me to this point.*

His perception of time slowed but not his velocity.

He slammed into the ground with the force of a falling star.

***

His tongue tasted metallic blood. *My blood.* He couldn't open his left eye. When he gingerly moved his hand to touch it, a blinding pain shot through his body. The pain left him gasping for breath, and blood streamed down his cheek.

Dante took the bottom hem of his robe and tore off a long, jagged piece of cloth. With a loud ripping sound, a long strip separated from the rest. He covered his bleeding left eye and tied it around his head.

Groaning, he sat up. He was in the middle of a crater. With his good eye, he looked around, careful not to move too quickly.

The red that he always saw at Hell's Gate was still prevalent here. Sweat began forming on his forehead before he was even aware of the fact it was as hot as a summer's day. Squinting, he peered at the bleeding red sun that stained the sky.

Humans always believed Hell was a pit of fire. Well, they weren't entirely wrong.

He wiped his forehead. Sweat coated his body.

Around him was empty land. No trees, no plants, nothing. Just rocky ground and a red sky. Not even a sinner in sight. With all the sinners who entered Hell every day, he expected the entire place to be packed, elbow to elbow. Honestly, that was the most surprising part.

But how do I get out of here?

Sudden inspiration struck him and he reached back for his scythe. He was surprised to learn he still had it. No one took it from him. Was it oversight or intentional? Either way, he had to try.

He staggered to his feet. He stumbled as he tried to regain his balance. A part of him still felt like he was falling through the air. Standing made his eye throb again as more blood pumped through his veins. He gasped for breath again. Although, all things considered, he did pretty well for falling such a distance.

He gripped his scythe and made a huge sweeping motion—much bigger than he ever did before. A breeze ruffled his hair. But nothing happened. To make sure, he kept swiping at the air, trying to tear it apart. No matter how many times he did it, the end result was still the same. He was truly trapped here.

Sweat dripped down his face and his breaths were quick and fast. The only thing he was accomplishing was wearing himself out. Cursing, he strapped his scythe on his back. *Now this thing is even more useless.* He stood there, not sure what to do, so he studied the landscape once more.

In the distance, he saw a wall. Or at least, it appeared to be a wall. A man-made structure for sure. He had no idea what to do or where to go. The wall didn't look promising, but it was something. And something was better than nothing.

***

Dante hobbled, focused on reaching the wall. As he got closer, he saw the wall was made of rough stone that had been quickly built. *What was the hurry? And is the wall trying to keep something out or something in?*

Either way, he felt drawn to it, as if it held answers. *Someone made the wall, right? So someone must be there.* That's what he told himself, anyway.

And so he trudged on the uneven ground through the blistering heat, sweating and aching.

But it wasn't just a wall. There was an opening. He steered toward it.

And in the opening stood a gigantic three-headed dog. But to call it a dog didn't give it the credit it deserved. Dante gulped as he tilted his head skyward, locking eyes with the monstrous beast.

Its paws were the length of Dante's whole body. Each snarling head could easily be seen over the high stone wall. Even the sun itself seemed to be blocked by the immense living shadow towering over him.

Fear gripped him. Every nerve ending in his body was telling him to run. But one look at the dog's huge, powerful legs told him fleeing wasn't an option. Not in Dante's state. Locked in place, he could only stare at the beast.

"Are you entering?" The growl was low and deep as if the ground itself had spoken.

He opened his mouth but he was unsure of what to say. He was certain if he said the wrong answer, it would be the last thing he would ever say.

His left eye throbbed again as adrenaline shot through him. What should he say? He wanted to go inside. If that was wrong, then so be it.

He sucked in his breath and answered, "Yes."

The dog looked at him, which was saying something because all three heads gave him their full attention. The heads dipped down to meet Dante's eyes.

"Are you sure?" The throats simultaneously grumbled with a deep sound Dante couldn't place. Was the dog growling at him? Maybe he did say the wrong answer.

"Yes," he repeated. His heart thumped in his chest so hard he was surprised the dog didn't comment on it.

The rumbling in the three throats continued to grow louder until it spilled out of their jaws in a barking sound. Dante jumped, but the dog only said, "You may pass."

Is he messing with me? Dante wondered if he walked around the dog, it would devour him anyway. But he didn't know what else to do, so subconsciously holding his breath, he stepped around the towering beast and walked through the opening.

He found himself in a courtyard, flanked by walls. The courtyard was empty except for a group of sinners huddled at the far side, away from the dog. They stared at him, eyeing his black robe and scythe slung on his back. *Not many reapers here, I'm sure.*

One man with squinty eyes glared at him. The man's expression made Dante stop in his tracks.

"You fool!" the man spat.

"Excuse me?" Dante asked.

"We're all trying to get out of here," the man said, waving his hand at the rest of the group. "And you just waltz right in here. Who wants to enter the City of Dis?"

"Wait, what?" *What's the City of This?*

"What an idiot," another man said, shaking his head.

Dante didn't fully comprehend what happened. Looking back at the massive dog, he realized the rumbling in its throats was laughter. A rush of embarrassment fell over him. *That stupid dog was laughing at me. And now I'm worse off than I was before.*

Between the dog and the wall, he caught a snippet of the world outside. Where it was just rocky ground and nothingness. Somehow, that was closer to escape than where he was now.

He turned back to the group of men. They were completely absorbed in conversation, ignoring Dante.

He cleared his throat. "So, how do you escape this place then?"

A few men darted their eyes toward Dante, but the melody of conversation never wavered. So Dante tried again, repeating his question louder.

The man with the squinty eyes gave him another hard look.

"I'm not telling a *reaper*," he said with venom in his voice. "You're the reason I'm here in the first place."

Dante frowned, feeling the sting of the man's words.

"I've never seen you before," he protested.

The man shrugged. "You're all the same to me." He turned his back on Dante and continued talking like he was never interrupted.

Dante opened his mouth but no sound came out. For an instant, he was transported back to The Council Room. Didn't he resign himself to an eternity in Hell in rebellion for sending sinners to this very place? And here were sinners, not caring, and worse, being spiteful toward him. It was like with the angels. They only saw him as a reaper, nothing more.

In that moment, he felt the first real ping of regret. *Maybe I really did make a mistake*, he thought as he stood there, being ignored by the very people he wanted to help. *What if Alex doesn't want anything to do with me either?*

"Let's go." An excited whisper from the group pulled Dante back into the present.

The group of sinners all ran toward the three-headed dog.

And they called me an idiot? Dante crossed his arms.

The men split up. A few ran right while others veered left. The rest sprinted straight at the dog. As they spread out, the dog snapped and snarled at them.

Apparently, they thought they could ambush the dog and overwhelm it by sheer numbers. The hope seemed to be that the dog couldn't get all of them and a lucky few would slip by. But they greatly underestimated the beast.

The dog's multiple jaws snapped in three different directions. Each bite swallowed a man whole. His tail swung around and pushed back the others who were trying to make a break for it. The men flew back, thrown on the ground like rag dolls. Stumbling to their feet, they realized the error of their ways and ran away from the dog, back toward the city.

It didn't matter to the dog. It leaped forward with such height and strength the wind rushed off of it as it soared over him. The dog landed and made the whole ground quake. The shockwave sent the fleeing men to their knees. Screaming, their faces twisted in terror as they gaped at the beast. They raised their arms over their heads in a pathetic attempt to shield themselves.

And then they were gone.

In one bite, it was like they never existed at all.

Dante stood there—the only one left. The dog sniffed in Dante's general direction and padded back to its spot at the gate.

Then it was silence. So quiet that he heard his heart hammering in his chest. He didn't realize sinners could still die in Hell.

Where did they go from here?

Chapter 9

A shriek froze Dante in place. Its eerie voice was filled with malice. A woman-like body, sleek and dark, flew above him as her bat wings spread out, riding the wind. She locked eyes with him and smiled. A jagged, twisted smile revealing fangs.

Dread welled up inside of him.

The creature kept flying toward the center of the city. It was too much hope that nothing would come of it.

The sun was scorching and sweat poured off of him. His throat was so parched he didn't even have saliva to swallow. And he had nothing to drink. There was no way he was going to escape Hell—let alone this city—without getting some water first.

Heading toward the city, he realized he was going in the same direction as that winged monster. But there was no helping it. Behind him was the three-headed dog. He was screwed, no matter which way he went.

Before, the ground was pressed dirt but now it became cobblestone. The stones were irregular and some jutted out at odd angles. One uneven stone caught his foot and sent him flying to the ground. Next thing he knew, he was staring straight into the hollow eye sockets of a human skull. Cursing, he flew back. And felt his hands brush up against another odd cobblestone. A skull blankly gaped at him with broken teeth.

His eyes widened as the realization hit him. The ground wasn't made up of stones at all. He was sitting on rows and rows of human skulls. Following the line of skulls, he slowly lifted his eyes to the center of the city.

How many? How many thousands of sinners have been buried here? His sweat turned cold despite the heat.

Another shriek penetrated his ear drums. The woman-like monster flapped above him and perched on top of the wall. She looked knowingly at him and smirked. This time, her fangs were stained with blood.

Unlike the three-headed dog, it didn't seem like this creature could talk, but it definitely was trying to communicate. Following the monster's gaze, he noticed the wall surrounded the whole city. And it would be really easy to scale the walls since they were made with many bumpy stones perfect for footholds. *So why even try to get past the dog when I could climb the wall?*

As if it heard his thoughts, the woman-like creature shrieked in reply and released a body from its talons. The ragged body landed with a thud next to him. Startled, Dante scrambled to his feet. This sinner didn't just die. The body had been ripped apart. Parts of bones stuck out at odd angles. *Was this another cobblestone in the making?*

He gazed at the cobblestone road again. *Were these all sinners who tried to escape this city?* He met the eyes of the monster. *What is this place?*

This was definitely a warning for him. That was for certain. If he was going to get out of this city, he wasn't going to escape by climbing the wall. He would have to find another way.

The monster preened her wings, evidently proud of the fact she made her point clear.

Since he got the hint, he didn't want to stick around. Dante trudged toward the city, away from the monster. He made sure to stay far away from the wall. As he walked, he felt a rush of wind behind him. Too late—the monster was upon him. Sharp talons ripped the back of his robe as the weight of the woman-like creature threw him to the ground. He gasped as he once again came face-to-face with the dark holes of a skull.

Is this the end of me?

The monster laughed—a high-pitched, eerie sound—and flew off, away to the center of the city. The monster was toying with him. And he was sure that it would be back.

Sighing, he got to his feet again. This place was nothing like he expected. And so many monsters he never knew existed. He had barely arrived and there was so much he didn't know. And somewhere there was a fallen angel who almost escaped Hell. If he really wanted to get out of here, he needed to find her. She obviously knew how to escape.

At the moment, the streets were empty, an eerie calm. As he walked, his eyes swept side to side. He was on high alert for anything unusual.

The buildings were barely standing. Huge cracks tore through the plaster, revealing rotten wooden beams. Pieces of plaster tumbled down in small avalanches as he wandered past. He peered into a few open windows but was hesitant to enter any of the structures. The force of opening and closing the door would probably be enough to collapse the whole place on him. Besides, everything here seemed abandoned.

He continued on as he was forced to make more sharp turns at forks in the road. At first, he tried to keep track of how many lefts and rights he made, but after the first few turns, he gave up.

A whip cracked. He stopped, listening hard. A scream of pain followed. Well, he wasn't alone anymore, but it didn't sound good. He wasn't confident in his abilities to fight off anything that came his way.

Trying to understand the direction of the sounds was hard because all the buildings were close together, making it echo everywhere. The noise bounced off walls and made plaster spray onto the cobblestones. He dodged the chunks as they tumbled around him.

He guessed which way to go, but really, he was just looking for places where the walls weren't crashing down. Rounding a corner, he stopped short, almost running into—

"You there!" A scaly body turned, his jaundice yellow eyes narrowing at him.

It was a demon. *Yep, I'm in trouble.*

Dante wasted no time. He ran.

***

Blindly, he kept turning corners, his feet pounding. He waved around buildings collapsing as he passed them. He didn't know where he was going exactly. Only when he put enough distance between him and the demon did he slow his pace. Glancing behind him, he didn't see anyone following him. For a moment, he could breathe.

He wanted to find Alex or that mysterious fallen angel. But he would also settle for finding some water. His throat was dry and his lips cracked from the lack of moisture. He even stopped sweating so much from the lack of water in his body.

He zigzagged through the maze that was the city. Buildings seemed to have been put up quickly and at random, with no thought of how things would work together. There was even a building that had a huge base but had to narrow at an odd angle to account for the arch running next to it.

He didn't know what purpose all these buildings served. Dante snuck a look inside a broken window, trying to make sense of the shadows. There wasn't any furniture. The door frames didn't have any doors. Everything inside and out was the same dry-bone color. It made it seem like the entire city was a skeleton. No one lived here—not anymore.

Pausing, he stopped at the sight of an up-turned book with the aged pages fanning out. As he picked it up, the gold lettering on the cover flaked off. It was hard to read, but it said, "Cecelia Morningstar." Curiosity gripped him. Turning to the first page, he read:

In the beginning, there were whispers. Darkness clung to the corners of Heaven, and there, whispers thrived. If you wandered too close, the whispers latched onto you, slithering in your ears. You could try to shake them off, but words are powerful. More powerful than any of us realized.

I suppose we should have known. We had seen firsthand how God brought forth light from darkness, something from nothing, with just a word. The Word of God was powerful. Such words brought forth life, to conquer death.

In the Garden of Eden, a snake whispered into the ears of Adam and Eve. Such powerful words. With those words, they chose to defy God and eat the Fruit of Forbidden Knowledge. After all God had done and given to Adam and Eve, only to be thwarted by a few simple words from a reptile.

What are words? We throw them around so carelessly. In a breath, we change the course of history, our future, our destinies. And yet, we don't think about those words. But words become a part of us.

And then, worst of all—words become action.

This is our story. We are the Fallen.

Dante breathed, taking in the words. *So it's true. The Fallen are here.* The stories never seemed real to him growing up—it was just a scary story to frighten children into listening. But it was very real.

Not many pages remained. Many crumbled in his hand, turning to dust. He lamented the lost words, wishing he knew what secrets they held. He could only read the last faded page:

Lucifer wears a gold crown, adored on top of his golden head. Truly, he is the King of the City of Dis. His silver tongue has led us here. Fallen though we may be, we rejoiced to be here with him. He told us we would build something greater than Earth or even Heaven. We may have been banished here—he told us—but that doesn't mean we can't enjoy ourselves. He promised us the wine would flow in our glasses and the bread would fill our baskets. It held true for a time.

We built this city on the backs of sinners. It was a part of their punishment—that is what we told ourselves. It was right to do so. They were just sinners after all. They became our slaves.

And so, the City of Dis was made. It is a sprawling city, huge and impressive. Building soared into the sky. Pointed arches and columns decorated the structures. Tops of towers were gilded in gold.

But there weren't many of us. Not nearly enough to fill an entire city. So most of the buildings lay empty, like hollow boxes. How fitting.

Then soon, everything we built began to crumble. At first, cracks appeared. Then, walls crumbled. Buildings collapsed. No matter what we tried to do, we couldn't stop it. It was like the whole world was crumbling. It appears you cannot build on top of a mountain of lies. And it seems like Lucifer's lies finally caught up to us. Everything here is fake. This decaying city is a pale comparison to the Kingdom of Heaven.

This is a place of suffering—a place of ruin and destruction. To think anything different is folly. Even I feel like I am fading away, poisoned by this dreadful place. How much longer can I last?

He accidentally breathed too hard and the page disintegrated. The words drifted away in the wind. A sadness tormented him as he set the book back down. *No one else will be able to read this. The words die with me.* And whoever wrote this may be dead by now. *How much longer can I last?* It was a question for Dante, too.

Silent and alone, he was lost in the crumbled city and in his thoughts.

Chapter 10

Sighing, he continued his trek. He wasn't finding anything and he was getting tired. For hours it seemed like it was just the blazing sun overhead, endless dilapidated buildings, and the horrible skull cobblestone road. How big was this city?

He paused for a moment, taking in the surroundings. Without thinking, he shoved his hands in his pockets. He found the loaf of bread he had stuffed in there this morning. Pulling it out, he stared at it as if it was the most foreign object he ever set eyes on.

This morning felt like an eternity ago. *Was it really a few hours ago that my whole life changed forever?* This morning he woke up in his own bed, talked to Tommy, and went to the Town Hall. Like every morning. But now his whole life was turned upside down and would never be the same.

He inspected the bread. Mold had grown all over it. They received a loaf fresh every morning and ate it on the same day. He was sure it was still the same day.

His stomach growled. Apparently, his body didn't care that there was mold on it. And the horrible thing was that this was the only food in the whole city. He hadn't seen anything that even closely resembled food this whole time.

But with his mouth being so dry, there was no way he would be able to swallow even one bite. So he trudged on, stuffing the bread back in his pocket, still searching for water.

As he continued walking, he heard a noise. The rushing sound was unmistakable—running water.

Finally, something is going right. Dante quickened his step, heading toward it. Sure enough, there was a river cutting through the streets.

The skull cobblestones ended as the banks sloped down, meeting the water.

The churning river was brown and gritty. It didn't look appetizing, but at the moment, he was too thirsty to care. He scurried down to the edge of the river. Careful not to fall in, he scooped it with his hands. He slurped it up, water dripping down his chin.

At first, he was drinking it too fast to notice, but as he scooped another handful, he gagged. Too late. He already swallowed some water. The oily water slid down his throat. Bile rose in his mouth. It was easily the most disgusting liquid he had ever tasted. The "gross" water he used to complain about tasted heavenly in comparison.

But he wasn't thirsty anymore. So there was that. His stomach growled again, reminding him about the moldy bread in his pocket. Sighing, he pulled the loaf back out. He really didn't want to eat it, but his stomach twisted and gurgled, demanding food.

Closing his eyes, he choked down the bread. It tasted stale and the texture was all off. It was chewy and parts of it were fuzzy. Nevertheless, he forced it down. It felt like a lump stuck in his throat. He examined the water warily. He needed to drink something but he really didn't want to. Groaning, he gulped another handful of water. It released the lump in his throat, but he shuddered as the slimy liquid squirmed in his stomach.

He breathed a sigh of relief when he was done eating and drinking. Despite how absolutely horrible that experience was, he felt a bit better to at least have something filling. *I will never complain about reaper food again.* But even as he thought it, he wondered if he really ever would get out of here. He knew he acted so sure of himself in front of The Council, but in reality, he had found Hell to be more than he bargained for. It was a dangerous place. He never felt safe. Even now, his eyes darted around, imagining the shadows as a demon or some other horrible creature lurking there.

Thinking of home pained him. He knew his father and mother were upset and he may never see them again to say he was sorry. Because he was sorry. As much as they annoyed him, he did love them.

But even now, he still didn't think he was wrong. The sinners may have turned their backs on him, but he wasn't here looking for praise. He was here because he didn't want to be a part of the system. *Why does Hell have to exist in the first place? Why does sin have to exist?*

A creaking noise broke Dante out of his thoughts. Before he knew why, his adrenaline pumped through his veins. It seemed there was no such thing as a good noise here.

A cart came into view, being pulled by sinners. All the sinners wore the same drab, gray cloth garment and a scowl on their faces. Behind them, a demon walked with a whip in his hand. The cart clattered and shook over the cobblestones. Its rusty wheels squeaked from the weight of stones and debris that it hauled.

He quickly retreated from the riverbank, running to the nearest building to hide. Turning a corner, he pressed himself flat against the building. The squeaking wheels stopped and the groans cried out. The snap of the whip sliced the air and screams of pain followed.

"Get up!" The whip cracked again. "Move it!"

Tired voices protested, but the demon only said, "Get up or I'll feed you to the dogs. They'll rip you limb from limb while you're still alive."

Shuffling followed and soon, the squeaking wheels began crying out again. *I guess that was the motivation they needed.* Dante assumed the demon was talking about the three-headed dog, but now he wasn't so sure. There might be others.

He needed to keep moving. It was too dangerous to stay in one place. Besides, he still had to find a way out of here. His luck was running out.

Chapter 11

The sun was high in the sky, never blinking, always watching with its scalding eye. Dante periodically glanced up, keeping track of it. He felt like he had been walking for days, but according to the sun, it was only hours.

He had been on the move in the heat and sun. His left eye throbbed in pain at every step, and sweat poured off of him. Not to mention his black robe was the worst color he could wear. The sun was baking him alive.

And he was no closer to finding the mysterious fallen angel. Or finding his own way of escaping. There had to be another way out of here besides going through the front entrance with the three-headed dog or trying to scale the walls watched by the evil winged-bat women.

So far, he found nothing.

He entered what had to be the city's center with gigantic, imposing architecture with soaring spears and long pointed arches decorated with intricate designs. The rest of the city was on the verge of collapse, but it was obvious a lot more care was put in here. Patches of plaster were whiter where it was still fresh, and any debris from crumbling structures had been cleaned up. Here and there, bright spots of color sparkled where statues and murals had been repainted.

He paused, inspecting one mural sprawled across the vast plaza. It depicted what had to be Lucifer with his golden hair and golden robe flying across a city. He was flying higher and brighter than the sun. Angels and demons had arms up to praise him while sinners cried in pain on the ground. *Very subtle.* Dante shook his head in disgust. *Lucifer really thinks highly of himself.*

Whips snapping were quickly becoming a common noise to hear. So were the screams of pain. And both sounds were close by.

The city center was more open with huge plazas and few buildings to hide behind. Dante felt exposed. His eyes darted around and rested on a huge, towering edifice. It looked important. It also looked like a good place to hide.

Half-running and half-jumping, Dante leaped up the steps to the building and threw open an enormous wooden door. As he pulled on the bronze handle, he glanced at the detailed carvings on the door. Even in his rush, he noticed angels carved on the surface with wings outspread. *Even here, I still have to deal with angels.*

He closed the door, surprised at how light it felt despite its size. Stepping inside, he found himself in a grand dining hall. The ceiling soared above him—what was left of it, anyway. The rest of the roof was open, exposing the red sky and hot sun.

In the sunrays, dust motes lazily danced. Long dining tables lined the walls and chairs were strewn about. The tables were still set for a party that had ended long ago. Dusty glasses of dried wine were cracked and busted. Plates were still full of figs, pomegranates, moldy cheese, and other food so rotted he couldn't tell what they were. The foul stench hit his nose, and the flies buzzed around him.

But at least he had a place to hide from the demons. At least he was alone.

Hands clapped.

The hairs on the back of his neck pricked. He felt for his scythe, feeling reassured by the handle.

Laughter filled the hall. A high-pitched hollow laugh that tore his insides.

A voice from the end of the hall called out, "What is a reaper who doesn't reap?" The voice sounded like a brass instrument, low, deep, and strong, but it carried a sinister tone.

A riddle. But really, who am I? If I'm not a reaper, what am I? Nothing? He never gave it a thought before. A chill set in. *Am I nothing now?*

He crept closer. Someone sat on a throne that was truly meant for a king with gold intricate swirls that framed the throne like a lion's mane. The figure wore a gold robe, each fold of cloth shimmering in the light. Golden hair crowned his head, and his curls framed his face. He smiled as Dante's eyes rested on his face. His lips stretched over his too perfect pearly white teeth.

"Lucifer." Dante spat his name like a curse.

Somehow that made Lucifer smile even more.

"I've been expecting you," he greeted as he rose from the throne.

Goosebumps prickled his arms. He had never met Lucifer before, but that part didn't matter. Everyone from Heaven to Hell and everywhere in-between knew him.

"How did you know I was here?" Dante asked.

"A little Fury told me." He grinned even wider, if that was possible.

Feeling like someone was watching him, he looked up. The evil winged-bat woman perched on the roof. The monster glared at him, sending shivers up his spine. *So that's a Fury.*

Lucifer floated closer, his wings fluttering.

"Get away from me." Dante recoiled.

"That's no way to talk to me. We are one and the same."

"Don't you dare compare me to you." Dante's hands shook. He wanted nothing more than to wring his too-perfect neck.

Lucifer opened his arms wide.

"When I first fell, I too was angry and bitter," Lucifer began, like he was imparting wisdom. "My heart was full of hate. I knew better than God—I still do—and I resented how I was banished to this wretched place." He waved vaguely around them. "Oh, I was so angry. I thought I would win. I whispered in ears and the other angels nodded. Soon, I had enough nodding to retaliate against the will of God. All of heaven was in turmoil. I thought I had a chance, you see. But I was ultimately banished." He frowned as he dropped into thought. Then he shook his head.

"But, why should I have to obey God? Why can't I follow my own path, my own destiny? I wanted to be independent, to do what I wanted to do. And what I wanted was to be god myself. So here I am, the god of the underworld." He threw his arms up as if he was triumphant.

Dante couldn't help but wonder if Lucifer had a point. *Isn't that what I'm doing? I'm rejecting my God-given duty to be a reaper and finding my own way?* But something about that didn't sit right with him. *Lucifer is the ultimate evil and if I'm siding with him, then what does that say about me?* Doubt squeezed his heart. *Does that mean I was wrong?* Echoes of screams filled his head as memories flashed before his eyes—memories of sinners sent to Hell, the very Hell God created. *No matter what, I can't go back to that.*

But what did it mean to reject God? Lucifer did and now what? He's stuck in Hell, no matter how he spins it. Yes, he has a throne, but everything is falling down around him. How is this better?

"Is this what you do all day? Just sit around in this empty, filthy place?" Dante asked, curious.

"No," Lucifer responded with such conviction it reverberated throughout the hall. "Soon, I will raze this place to the ground and build a new city—a better one that will put this all to shame. I will construct it better. And this time, it will not fail."

"Yeah? And how do you plan to do that exactly?"

His wings opened up, fluttering and expansive. The white wings caught the light, and they were dazzling. The huge room felt small in comparison.

"I do not have to explain myself to the likes of you." Lucifer raised his chin, looking down at Dante.

His words burned Dante. "You're not any better than me. We're both stuck in this shithole."

Lucifer scowled. "I thought you didn't want to compare us together."

Dante threw out his arms. "Well, we're both here, aren't we? The hierarchy in Heaven is null and void as far as I'm concerned. I'm tired of you angels always looking down on reapers."

"For good reason. You were only created to harvest souls to be judged. Reapers are too close to sinners."

"As opposed to now, where we're among them?"

"I am not among them—I rule over them. And you as well."

Dante surveyed the surrounding rubble. "You rule over ruins. There's only destruction here."

Lucifer's head jerked as if Dante's words slapped him. In a flash, he was upon Dante, squeezing his throat. Lucifer's eyes squinted with rage. Dante struggled to breathe as his feet dangled above the ground.

"You are nothing. Everything you did was for nothing. Nothing changed and nothing ever will," Lucifer spat.

He echoed Dante's earlier thoughts. Dante choked on his words. Those words suffocated him more than Lucifer's grip. He knew. Lucifer knew it was hard to hear. Lucifer wasn't feared for no reason. He saw Dante's darkest thoughts and used them against him. Despair clouded Dante's thoughts as his sight went black from the lack of air.

Proving his point, Lucifer released him. Dante fell to the ground, coughing. Dark spots in his vision slowly retreated from view as he gasped for breath. He still felt Lucifer's grip on his throat as if it had burned his skin.

Lucifer stepped back from him, watching. A grin appeared on his face again.

He thought he taught me a lesson. Showed me who was boss. Dante grimaced.

"I will make you bow to me."

The thought of Lucifer lording over him made Dante's blood burn with rage. "Never!" He scrambled to his feet.

Lucifer grinned wickedly. "Enough talk. I'll show you. And soon, you *will* bow to me."

A large rumble shook the building, collapsing the rest of the roof. Huge pillars fell around him. He scrambled out of the way as one huge column came hurling down on him.

He looked back at Lucifer, but he was gone. *Damn him.* The ground shook again. He stumbled as the ground continued to shake everything, rattling his bones. Another column collapsed on the dining table. Shattered wood flew. Ducking, he ran. He leaped over chairs and debris toward the entrance.

When he reached the outside, he thought he was safe. But it wasn't only the dining hall that was collapsing—it was the entire city. *Is this a part of Lucifer's plan? Is this how he is going to raze this entire place?*

Buildings crashed down around him, plaster raining in chunks. He had no idea where to go or how to get out of here. Every turn he made, it was just more walls, more buildings, more courtyards.

Dante was trapped in a maze with no way out.

Chapter 12

Behind Dante, a loud crack ripped through the air as a structure tumbled down. Pieces of plaster and stone rained down on him, particles spraying. The ground shook violently as he staggered. It was like a war zone. Chaos everywhere.

All the collapsing buildings kicked up dust like fog, covering the sky. Even the bright sun was dimmed by the haze. He could barely see, let alone tell where he was going.

Dizzy and disoriented, he stumbled around the debris. It was hard to breathe and he inhaled all the thick clouds of dust. It stuck to his throat and lungs. His parched throat stung, begging for a drop of water.

He scraped past a corner and caught sight of a silhouette through the dust, but that was enough to tell who it was. The outline of feathery wings was a dead give-away.

"Lucifer!" he choked out.

The angel halted at the name and turned toward him.

And then Dante saw the long, flowing hair. Not Lucifer's tight curls. This was someone else.

"Do not call me that," she commanded.

The angel came closer. It was the same girl who almost escaped Hell. He still remembered her wide golden eyes and the grip on his arm.

"It's you," he said, stunned. He had been searching for her and here she was.

"What does that supposed to mean?" She acted like she wanted to know but then started walking away.

Dante shrugged and fell in stride with her. "I was there when you almost escaped Hell."

She paused mid-step and stared at him. He felt exposed under her scrutiny. He was painfully aware his robe was ragged and coated with dust. His makeshift eye patch was still wrapped around his head. Blood and sweat streaked down his cheeks. And his scythe hung uselessly on his back.

"Oh, you're that reaper," she said, distracted. Her eyes flitted around, searching for something. "What are you doing here?"

"Trying to get out of here."

The ground shook. Dante and the angel both stumbled, trying to keep their footing.

"I as well. You did try to help me, even though it didn't work. Follow me, just don't slow me down."

She resumed her swift walking speed. Dante struggled to keep up.

"But how are you here?" He puffed out the question, already out of breath.

"I was born here."

"How is that possible?"

"And how is it possible for a reaper to be here? I've been here all my life and I've never seen such a thing. You must have done something really bad."

Dante scowled. "Yeah, I tried to save you."

"They punished you for that?"

"And because I stopped reaping souls."

"But you're a reaper."

"I'm well aware of that. But I didn't want to keep sending souls to Hell."

A group of sinners ran past, screaming for mercy.

She squinted at them. "I see your point."

The rumblings shook the ground, knocking down more walls. Structures cracked in half and tumbled down. The dust billowed into thick clouds. It felt as though the whole world was falling apart at the seams.

"How's this happening?" Dante asked.

"This is Lucifer's doing."

"Lucifer did say he was going to destroy the city and make it even better. But how is he doing this?"

"He is powerful," she said. She seemed to have a habit of stating something without further explanation. It was already getting annoying.

More stones crashed around them. He dodged the falling debris, instinctively putting his arms over his head. They ran forward. Everything in front of him was a haze of dust and debris. He didn't know how the angel saw where to go. But he was glad because he had no idea how to navigate this maze. It was endless.

She leaped nimbly over tall piles of rumble. Her wings fluttered mid-air. A thought struck him.

"Why are you walking when you have wings?" he asked as they continued to zig-zag around the rubble.

"Never you mind why," she said. Her lips pressed together, locking in her secrets.

Dante frowned. *There's more to her than just being a normal angel. What is she hiding?*

High up in the sky, wings stretched out, impossibly long. Against the hazy, dusty sky, Lucifer gleamed. The light reflected off of his golden curly hair and his magnificent, flowing robe, making him sparkle. He truly looked like a bright morning star. *A star to doom us all.*

As Lucifer raised his arms, violent tremors shook the whole city.

He's controlling the earthquake? He truly is powerful. Cold dread washed over Dante.

The shaking was even worse now. Tripping, falling, stumbling, Dante and the angel sprinted past walls falling down on them. They leaped over piles of stone that cluttered the streets as the ground gave way beneath them.

Huge cracks snaked the ground, yawning chasms opening to the darkness. He briefly wondered what was below. *Is there a deeper Hell?*

As if to answer him, the cracks turned molten red. Lava spilled out like blood pouring out of a wound. The heat came quick and intense. The cracks were becoming one as the lava oozed together, setting fire to anything it touched. Soon, smoke filled the air, joining forces with the dust. His left eye throbbed as he tried to squint into the haze.

Fiery lava surrounded them.

"Hey," he choked out. The sulfur stung his eyes and throat. "Are you sure you can't fly?" *Why can Lucifer fly but not her?*

"I can't," she breathed, a cry caught in her throat.

"Then how are we going to get out of here?"

The air was thick with smoke, and the heat baked him alive. As the lava slithered closer, they pressed together, running out of space. Fear rose within him. He had to think of something fast.

"Okay, so you can't fly for whatever reason. But you can move your wings, yes? I saw you earlier."

"Yes," she said, uncertain.

"So, get a running start and flap your wings as hard as you can to jump over this lava."

"And what about you?"

"Uh" was the intelligent reply from Dante.

The lava bubbled and glided over the rubble, coming straight toward them. Smoke rose in its wake. It was now or never.

She smiled grimly at him. "Hold on."

He didn't understand what she meant. Next thing he knew, she scooped him up like she was embracing him—*awkward*—and took a running leap over the liquid fire. The flames reached out like tendrils. She hit the ground and stumbled over debris. They both went tumbling. Dante landed on his back, cushioned by his scythe's handle jabbing him in the spine. He gasped and rolled over. He glanced where the lava was, ready to move out of the way.

The angel was sprawled out, still reeling from the fall. Dante squinted through the smog. Sweat dripped in his eyes, and the sulfur stung his nose. But even through the haze, he saw the lava flowing toward her, dangerously close. He scrambled over and dragged her away from the enclosing lava.

She whimpered as she tried to stand.

"What's wrong?" he asked.

"It's my ankle. I think it's twisted." She winced as she put pressure on her right foot.

"Can you walk at all?" He wasn't trying to be mean, but his voice came out gruffer than he meant to. All he could focus on was the lava pouring toward them from every direction. They still weren't safe.

"Of course I can," she said with determination. She tried to stand but wobbled on one foot.

Dante shook his head. "That isn't going to work."

***

Everywhere the lava flowed, the ground burst into flames. All the piles of rubble made for the perfect kindling. Smoke filled the air and his lungs. The ground shook, splitting open massive chasms that poured out more lava.

"Okay, you're going to have to tell me where to go," Dante said as he side-stepped a pile of debris engulfed in flames.

"I can't see anything. All I can see is your back."

"Do I really have to carry you like a baby?"

She sucked in her breath. Her lungs expanded against his shoulder.

"Yes, I suppose so," she admitted.

He paused for a moment to readjust her. It took longer than it should have because he had to account for her wings. Even though they were folded up, they were still huge. It was another minute of her wincing in pain and him finding a way to hold her and not hurt her wings.

"These damn things are useless anyway," he grumbled.

"So is your scythe and you didn't hear me complaining about getting whacked repeatedly in the face with it."

"Okay, fine. How do we get out of here?" he asked. He looked down at her. He realized how close she was to him, and she gazed back at him with her sparkling golden eyes with long lashes. His breath caught.

She quickly turned away and pointed. "That way." Her cheeks flushed.

He followed her finger. It didn't seem any different from the rest of the smoky haze.

"Are you sure?"

"Just do it," she snapped.

He sighed. "I'm still following orders from an angel," he muttered to himself.

"I heard that."

He didn't reply because the lava was fast approaching them. He had no choice but to go in the direction she pointed to. He ran even though he could only see one step in front of them. She bounced in his arms, and he tightened his grip to make sure she didn't fall.

She occasionally would redirect him where to go, and he blindly followed orders. Soon, they came upon the river Dante passed earlier, which felt like a lifetime ago.

"I remember this," he said. "We are going back the way I came into the city."

"Yes, I told you this was the right way."

"But that means we are also heading back to that three-headed dog," he said with a frown.

"You mean Cerberus? Yes, that's the only way out of the city."

"But if the whole city is collapsing, doesn't that mean the walls around the city are crumbling, too?"

She sighed. "Even if the walls came down, we would have to deal with the demons and the Furies. Out of all of them, I'll take my chances with Cerberus."

"But they can't be around the entire perimeter," Dante argued, refusing to go another step.

"Lucifer gave them all orders to make sure no one leaves the city alive. Besides, they all can fly. We can't. And that's a huge disadvantage."

"Ah, so we definitely can take down a gigantic three-headed dog. I get it," Dante said sarcastically. "Good thing you can't walk and I can't see out of one eye. Yeah, let's take our chances. Uh-huh."

"Do you have a better idea?"

"Nope."

"Then let's keep going."

With a sigh, he continued through the smoke and dust.

Chapter 13

At the edge of the city, the destruction wasn't as bad. Some of the buildings were still vertical, almost normal looking in their original, dilapidated state. The smoke wasn't as thick either, and the fresh air felt cold after inhaling the hot fumes for so long.

"Okay, keep going straight now," she said.

"Yes, your majesty."

He was being sarcastic, almost joking, but his words sparked anger in her eyes—the same as when he accidentally called her Lucifer.

"Call me Sophia," she said, grimacing.

"I guess this is time for the introductions. I'm Dante."

The buildings gave way to an open area. All that was in front of them was the three-headed dog. *Cerberus*, Sophia called him. The name didn't fit him. There was no fierceness in the name, no sense of horror, no whisper of certain death. Because that's what this dog really was. Dante stopped. His legs were no longer willing to carry him any closer to the humongous beast that blotted out the sun.

Cerberus was busy eating one helpless sinner while another ran, trying to get past him. He too got gobbled up.

A whole group of sinners rushed at the dog, trying to overwhelm him. Cerberus snatched up three sinners and then used his tail to swipe the others to keep them inside until he could devour them too.

Dante gulped.

Once again, he wished Sophia could fly. How easy this all would be. *What good is it to have an angel if she's not even useful?*

A sinner hung out to the sides, watching with disinterest. It was the guy with dark hair and a narrow chin—Alex. It felt like forever ago when Dante reaped his soul. When Dante had no idea he would be joining him here.

"How's Hell treating you?" Dante asked casually as he slid next to him. Dante let Sophia down, so she hobbled on one foot.

"Not as great as you, apparently." Alex smirked. "Got yourself a girlfriend, huh?"

Dante didn't know whether to feel indignant or laugh. He wanted to deny any indication of a relationship with an angel, but he was also amazed how nonchalant Alex was in the face of everything. Alex acted like it was no big deal to be in Hell, to meet up with the very reaper who brought him here, and to stare down a huge three-headed dog.

Dante did the best he could by laughing while shaking his head.

"Are you trying to escape, too?" Dante asked him.

"No, I love it here," Alex answered, his words dripping with sarcasm.

"Well, we're getting out of here," Dante said, nodding toward Sophia.

Sophia frowned. "I'm so happy you found a friend down here, reaper, but we really need to keep moving. This part of the city won't last long either."

"You sure make a lot of demands for someone who can't even walk."

"You weren't complaining before when I navigated us out of the city center," she said with her hands on her hips.

"Okay, sure. Then enlighten me, angel," Dante said. "Tell me how to get past this gigantic three-headed dog that can eat me in one bite."

Alex shook his head. "You guys are so precious."

Dante and Sophia both refuted his claims.

"Okay, okay," Alex said, putting his hands up. "So what do we do about the dog?"

"I'm thinking," she said. Her eyes scanned the area as if she was looking for inspiration.

"You know, there is a story that Cerberus was defeated once. The man was so strong he only used his bare hands," Alex said thoughtfully.

"That is a myth," Sophia retorted.

Dante gazed at the beast. *So many monsters here. And I've run away from all of them. But now this one stands in my way. This time, I will not run—not anymore. I'm tired of running.*

Dante reached for his scythe. He didn't see any other way. Adrenaline jolted through his veins like lightning. His body was ready for action. *Yes, let's do this.*

"You're really going to fight that thing?" Alex's eyebrows shot up.

Dante didn't answer. He walked up to the three-headed gargantuan beast that ate souls for breakfast. The middle head stared down at him as it blew its hot breath on him. It opened all of its jaws. The tongues rolled out with globs of slobber dripping down. He looked up at the wrong time. One big drop of slobber fell on his head. The sickeningly warm goo slid down, absorbing into his hair, running down his neck in hot, thin rivers before finally getting soaked into his robe.

"Gross," he said.

Cerberus's multiple fangs gleamed as he opened his mouth wider. He made a deep rumble in the back of his throats. Apparently, he found this funny.

Dante brandished the scythe in front of him. "If you don't let us pass, then I'll have to kill you," he said, raising his voice to make sure the dog heard him high above.

Cerberus laughed again, but Dante stood firm.

"Foolish little reaper. I bet you wish you never entered the City of Dis." The three heads spoke at once. It created a chanting sound, low and gravelly.

"I wish for a lot of things," Dante admitted. "But right now, I wish for you to let us pass."

"I cannot let you. You are a sinner."

"But I haven't done anything wrong," he said, frustration tinged in his voice.

"You refused to do your duty. I am fulfilling mine."

Cerberus was stuck in Hell for no other reason but to do his duty. Dante felt a pang of sympathy.

"Man, it's going to suck when I defeat you."

"Oh?"

The "Oh" was a long, cascading foul breath. The kind of foul breath that was created from the smell of thousands of souls reeking on its teeth.

Dante gagged.

And he barely missed the dog's gnashing teeth. Falling back, he realized the breath was a distraction.

Another head came barreling down on him. Dante swiped at it with his scythe. The curved blade whistled through the air. The head jerked back in time, making Dante wide open for an attack.

The scythe was great for harvesting souls. Not so great as a weapon. And he never needed to fight before. To say Dante was outclassed by Cerberus was a huge understatement.

All the heads came in for an attack. Fangs out. Mouths wide. Cerberus was going in for the kill. Dante swung back in a wide arc. The blade sliced through the first snout, showering blood everywhere. The other two heads dodged his blade.

The drops of blood fell on him like rain, streaking his face. He stumbled as he wiped it out of his one good eye, struggling to see.

Cerberus's heads lunged again. Dante stepped back, swinging wildly. The cloth around his neck tightened as his feet were lifted from the ground. Dante dangled like a mouse caught in the clutches of a cat. Another head ripped the scythe out of his grip, sending it flying to the ground far below.

Dante was caught, unarmed, and defenseless.

"This is the end, reaper," Cerberus growled.

Dante was so high up he towered above everything. Beyond the walls, it was a desert, devoid of life. Then, at the very end of the horizon, a mountain expanded to the sky, shooting straight up. The mountain range stretched all the way around, across his whole view. He understood now. He had fallen into a pit—Hell was just a gigantic pit.

"Cerberus! Let him go!" Sophia shouted below. Even from up here, her voice commanded respect.

The jaws that held Dante stayed silent, but the other two heads responded.

"Stay out of this, fallen angel."

"You will listen to me. On the order of Lucifer, the Morning Star, the Shining One, the Leader of the Fallen, and the King of the City of Dis."

The dog gave a throaty laugh. "How can you make such a claim?"

Sophia straightened her shoulders and lifted her chin.

"I am Sophia Morningstar, Lucifer's daughter."

If Cerberus wasn't holding him, Dante was sure he would have fallen to the ground in disbelief. Sophia's words echoed in his head: *I was born here.* It was all starting to make sense.

Dante saw the angel in a new light. He realized why he accidentally referred to her as Lucifer. There was a striking resemblance in their golden hair and marble skin.

But right now, he didn't care she was Lucifer's daughter. Right now, she was his salvation, rescuing him from the jaws of death.

Cerberus unceremoniously opened his jaw, allowing Dante to fall. He dropped to the ground like a rock.

Groaning, Dante got to his feet.

"And you will let us pass," Sophia commanded.

"Very well," Cerberus said. "But hear this, Lucifer's daughter: Never interfere again. You are messing with forces which you know nothing of."

Sophia's face was set in stone, unreadable. Not saying another word, she marched right out of the city. Well, more like hobbled, but she took it in stride.

Dante scrambled to get his scythe and followed her with Alex close behind him.

Chapter 14

They filed out of the City of Dis with the huge three-headed dog, staring them down as they passed. Cerberus growled, but he didn't move.

But it wasn't just Dante, Alex, and Sophia. Hearing footsteps behind him, Dante turned to see more gray-robed sinners of all ages following close.

"Where did they come from?" Dante asked, bewildered. They weren't there when he was fighting Cerberus. Of course, he wasn't really paying attention to anything else when he thought he was about to die.

Alex shrugged. "They came out of the woodwork when Sophia ordered the dog to let us through. They must've been hiding, waiting for their chance." He looked meaningfully at Sophia. "Speaking of which, why didn't you tell the dog to heel in the first place? There was no reason for the reaper to fight at all."

"Dante," he interjected lightly. "My name's Dante."

"My bad," Alex said, not taking his eyes off Sophia.

Sophia kept her eyes pointed straight ahead. A scowl formed on her lips. "Any time I have to be reminded of who I am is torture. And when you're trying to escape, it's not in your best interest to draw attention to yourself." Her eyes flitted to Dante. "It's just that you looked so pitiful that I finally had to say something."

Dante opened his mouth to retort something about being the only reason she was even alive from a burning city when he was rudely interrupted.

A sinner ran ahead of Dante and flung herself down on the rocky ground in front of Sophia. Her torn robe and frizzled hair made her look wild with desperation.

"Angel! You're so merciful. You've led us out of the city and away from death! Thank God! He hasn't forsaken us!" The woman clung to the hem of Sophia's white robe, crying with relief.

"There is no God here," Sophia said, her voice wavering. "And even though we are out of the city, we are still trapped in Hell."

But it was like Sophia never said anything at all. The sinners flocked to the angel. They fell to their knees around her, praising her and God. With her wings fluttering at her sides, her flowing white robe, and her tumbling golden hair, she looked like everyone's ideal image of an angel.

Sophia opened her mouth to speak but couldn't. Tears streamed down her face. She gazed at everyone surrounding her in amazement.

The people looked at her like she was their messiah.

"Save us," they cried.

"I can't." Sophia shook her head. "I don't know if I can escape this place myself."

Dante watched Sophia and the sinners. Hope shone on the sinners' faces. The same hope he had. He thought he was a goner when Sophia saved him from Cerberus. And the only reason he thought he could escape was because of her too. He had seen her at Hell's Gate. She had been so close to actually getting out of here. And this time, they could do it. Dante felt a surge of hope.

Dante stepped forward. "We can help them," he said to Sophia.

She turned toward him, tears glistening in her eyes.

Dante addressed the crowd. "We're searching for a way to escape Hell. Come with us if you want."

Sophia's eyes shone. The sinners clung to her more, as if touching her robes made the idea tangible.

"What are you doing? How can you give them false hope?" she asked across the crowd.

Dante stood firm. "Down here, hope is all we have."

***

All the sinners—all fifteen of them—whole-heartedly agreed to go with them. *What other choice do they have?* It was odd having so many people with him. He was used to being alone. And now, not only was he surrounded by people, they were also looking to him to lead. He had never been a leader before. The closest he ever came was when he led Tommy into a tunnel he had discovered, only to run away screaming while bats screeched in his ears.

Outside the city, the sun was back in full force, beating down on them. Dante was drenched in sweat. A breeze would come through every once in a while, but it offered no real relief. The winds came from the city and carried hot air and smoke, reminders of the destruction behind them. The rocky ground was uneven and hard to walk on, forcing everyone to move slowly and carefully. Sophia refused to be carried anymore. Now there was no hurry, even she could keep up while hobbling on her ankle. Which was fine with Dante because he didn't have any energy left in him after his fight with Cerberus.

The praises that the sinners had sung faded on their lips. They marched on in silence, focusing only on the mountains ahead. The goal was to get to the mountains and climb up them to escape. That was the plan, anyway.

Dante found himself next to Sophia.

"So, why are you escaping?" he asked.

She sucked in her breath as she put weight on her ankle. "Do you really have to ask?"

He watched her for a moment. She was still a mystery to him. He was trusting her but he still didn't know anything about her.

"Actually, I do. Why isn't Lucifer's daughter back there, building a new city with him?"

She grimaced at Lucifer's name, but she didn't answer. She focused on her step as she hobbled over stones jutting up from the ground. The silence extended to the point where Dante wasn't sure if she was ever going to answer.

"I'm done," she said finally, as if that made any sense.

"Done with what?"

She waved her hand vaguely. "With all of it. I don't want to be a part of it anymore. I don't want to wake up to the sounds of pain. I don't want to see demons whipping sinners. I don't want to feel the crunching of bones under my feet." Her voice wavered like she might cry. "And I don't want to rule the city when my father passes."

"To rule?" Dante repeated in disbelief.

"Yes. He wants me to take his place. That's why he's destroying the city. So he can have a better one built for me to rule—to carry out his legacy."

"Wow, that sucks." Dante didn't know what else to say. He wasn't expecting that. He understood what it was like to have people expect you to keep the status quo you didn't agree with. But even he wasn't expected to live up to someone else's legacy. He was just a reaper. Not the son of anyone important, like the leader of the Fallen Angels.

He noticed how Sophia was walking even worse now as she puffed through the pain. "You could hold on to my shoulder if you want," he said.

"It's fine, really."

"It doesn't seem fine to me."

"I will need to bear pain."

The way she said it, it was like it would be this way forever. He stared at her as if suddenly she would unlock all her secrets. Everything she said sounded like a riddle, if only he could figure her out.

***

They continued to cross the rocky desert. Only dead trees dotted the landscape. As they passed underneath one particularly huge and twisted tree, the bony branches grasped at them. Thorns snagged

Dante's robe, yanking him back. Everything about this place tried to stop him. He tugged at the branch, struggling to free himself. With a crack, the branch gave way and fell lifeless to the ground. Dante shivered despite the heat.

He resumed walking, but he kept looking over his shoulder. He wondered if anyone was following them. Surely someone would have noticed them by now. It wasn't like it was hard to miss a whole group of people slowly moving across an open desert. But all he saw was flames and smoke inside the city.

Alex hurried up to him, matching Dante's speed.

"You checking to see if they're coming after us, huh?" Alex asked.

Dante masked his concern, giving a shrug. "It seems too easy, you know?"

Alex grinned. "You're not used to this, are you?"

Dante shook his head in confusion. "Used to what, exactly?"

"Running from the law, being on the bad side. I can see how nervous you are—always looking over your shoulder." Alex laughed to himself, apparently remembering something.

Dante frowned, realizing why Alex was here. "Well, I haven't been good either. I'm here, too."

Alex cocked his head, side-eyeing him. "Yeah, I was wondering about that. I didn't even know reapers could go to Hell."

"I didn't know either, but I sure found out." Dante wasn't sure why but that made him laugh. Maybe it was relief after all this craziness. He realized he had been walking and running around—not to mention fighting—since he Fell, which felt like a lifetime ago.

"So what are you here for, anyway? Don't tell me it's because you gave that angel lip."

"No, that gave me ten years of silver cases. That means only taking old people's souls."

Now it was Alex's turn to be confused. "And that's a punishment?"

"Yeah, it would be like you having to work in a retirement home for ten years."

"No, thanks," Alex said quickly.

"Exactly."

Alex laughed. "So then, what was it?"

Dante focused on the mountains ahead, not meeting Alex's eyes. He didn't know why, but he felt a bit embarrassed to tell him. "I refused to send sinners to Hell. Apparently, that's a big no-no."

"You sent me to Hell," Alex pointed out.

"Yeah, it was soon after that," Dante said, ducking his head.

"Oh, okay. Thanks for that, by the way."

Alex scowled and Dante felt a pang of guilt.

But Alex laughed and slapped Dante on the back. "You take everything too seriously. I'm just messing with you. I told you before it was my fault. I know what I did."

Dante wondered what Alex did and why he was so sure he would go to Hell for it. But something on Alex's face made Dante leave his questions on his lips. Alex had a faraway look in his eyes, lost in thought.

Sophia wobbled over, stubborn as ever.

"Reaper—" she started to say.

"Dante," he interrupted.

She sighed and continued. "We need to find a place to stop for the night. It will be too dangerous to continue after dark."

He wasn't sure why she was coming to him about this, but it seemed he had established himself as some kind of leader.

Dante took in the surroundings. The sun dipped down lower, casting long shadows. Soon, the sun would disappear behind the mountains. And they were nowhere near the mountains. The land stretched out, plain and deserted. Only a scattering of rocks and dead trees broke up the nothingness.

Where are we going to find a safe place to rest? There isn't any.

"Well, here is good," Dante said, shrugging.

"We will have to stand guard," Sophia said. She surveyed the land, looking for something but not seeing it. "The hellhounds come out at night."

Chapter 15

The shadows reached farther over the ground, like long, dark fingers taking hold over the land. The sun fell behind the mountains, taking its heat with it. Dante shivered as he felt the sudden change in temperature. Soon, the land would be plunged into darkness. This was Dante's first night in Hell.

"Hellhounds?" Dante repeated, his heart pounding.

"Yes, I'm sure you're wondering why there aren't more sinners here. That's because many get eaten. We aren't the first ones to escape the City of Dis. Many more have tried and failed." Sophia got quiet. Her head bowed as if she was remembering something.

"How can you die in Hell?" Alex asked. He sat on a large rock with his elbows on his knees. "I mean, isn't this it? I'm already dead."

Sophia also sat amongst the rubble. She rubbed her ankle before responding. "I hope you don't find out," she said.

"But I want to know. That's why I'm asking."

Dante watched Sophia. She had a lot of secrets she kept close to her chest. *What else are you not telling us?*

"Angel," said one of the sinners. This sinner was a young girl, not much older than Dante. She had thin brown hair and freckles sprinkled on her cheeks. Clasping her hands, she nervously stepped closer to Sophia. "The others and I were wondering if there was any food or water nearby. Some of us are near exhaustion. Please help us."

Sophia pursed her lips. Dante knew as well as she did there was nothing for miles around. But to simply say that was too harsh to hear.

"What's your name?" Sophia asked. Dante wondered if she was stalling.

The girl smoothed her hair. "Eva."

Sophia smiled sweetly. "Eva, I know you are suffering now. But soon, we will escape this place, and you will have all the food and drink you could ever want."

Eva's eyes grew wide, and a smile spread across her face. She clapped her hands. "Thank you, angel. You are truly God's gift from Heaven."

Sophia's eyes darkened at the mention of Heaven, but her sweet smile never wavered.

Eva didn't appear to notice the change in Sophia's face. She only focused on what she wanted to hear. And with that, she returned to the others to tell them what Sophia had said.

"I thought you didn't want to give them false hope," Dante said. He didn't mention how impressed he was with Sophia's handling of the situation. Of course, Lucifer was grooming her to be ruler.

Sophia kept her eyes focused on the distance. "False hope is all I can give."

***

The shadows deepened, but some light still stuck around even though the sun itself was gone. Everyone took this time to rest before night set in. They didn't have any food or water, but to sit in the cooler twilight air was enough to feel refreshed.

They relaxed and talked amongst themselves. The sufferings from the day faded as the sun sank behind the mountains. For a moment, they could forget some of the pain they endured.

A howl pierced the air, and others matched it. Dante's heart raced as he jumped up. He couldn't tell where the sound was coming from, but it sounded close. He removed his scythe from his back and gripped it in front of him. All he could hope for now was the scythe would be more useful than it was with Cerberus.

"Stay together, all of you," Dante addressed the sinners. "Sit with your backs together, facing out in a circle. Call out if you see something."

"What's out there?" Eva asked.

"Hellhounds," Sophia answered grimly.

Alex stood with a particularly sharp rock. "I'm ready," he said in a firm voice.

Dante hid a smile. He had to hand it to Alex. He never let anything get him down. And it was nice to have someone to stand shoulder to shoulder with.

"So what are you going to do, angel?" Alex asked. "Can you tell the hellhounds to stand down, too?"

"No," she replied. "They only have one master."

And I suppose you won't tell us who that is. Another cryptic message. There were still more secrets to uncover. But those would have to wait for now.

Another howl. It sounded close—too close. His hair on the back of his neck stood up. He held his scythe at the ready and steadied his breathing.

Then he saw them. They were blacker than the gray shadows of dusk. Their eyes glowed red, as if fire burned within. And all their eyes were trained on them.

Dante's blood turned to ice. There was no way they could hold off so many. Sophia was injured, Alex had a rock, and the others were exhausted and unarmed. Dante wasn't faring much better. His left eye throbbed and his limbs felt heavy.

"Well, you wanted to find out what happens when you die in Hell," Dante said to Alex.

"Please don't tell me this is your motivational speech," Alex replied.

Dante grinned despite the impending doom. If he had to go down, he would rather go down swinging, facing his death head on.

Two fiery eyes loomed closer. Dante didn't wait for an attack. He swung his scythe as hard as he could, slicing the living shadow in front of him. The blade connected and stuck. A whimper escaped from the hellhound. He yanked it out of the beast.

A rock whizzed by, striking the dog. Another yelp of pain. The hellhound retreated. Its eyes grew smaller as it shrank away.

Alex knelt down to pick up another rock.

Of course, Dante thought. *The whole ground is littered with rocks.*

"Everyone! Grab a rock and throw them at the hellhounds!" Dante called to the others.

The dusk quickly waned to an inky black night. There were no stars or moon. All Dante could see were flaming eyes. More were appearing close together. They were surrounded by eyes like they were trapped in a demonic circle.

The sound of a rock whooshed by and landed aimlessly on the ground. With an ear-piercing howl, the hellhounds attacked at once.

Dante swung his scythe in a long arc. A shallow hit jarred his elbow. Before Dante could wind up another attack, a hellhound jumped on him. The unexpected weight pushed him down. His back crashed into the sharp rocks. He gasped for breath and gained a lung-full of foul sulfur smell as the dog bared down on him.

He couldn't see the teeth, but they gashed, snapping right in front of his face. By twisting his arm, he freed his weapon as he swore at the unwieldiness of it. Finally, he managed to turn the blade toward the beast. But before he could use it, the hellhound bit his left shoulder. Its fangs sunk into his flesh. Dante cried out in a gurgle of pain. He tried to push the dog off, but it only clenched tighter. Pain seared through his body while his shoulder blade felt like it was going to snap under the pressure of its jaw.

With his right hand, he thrusted the blade into the hellhound's shaggy neck. It didn't let go of his shoulder but it snarled in pain. Dante plunged the blade in further with all his remaining strength. The dog whimpered, and its jaw finally slacked. Dante pushed the beast off of him. Its eyes dimmed as life left it.

He scrambled to his feet, holding his shoulder. Warm liquid poured over his hand. There was a lot of blood, but he still gripped his scythe. The fight wasn't over yet—that was just one beast.

Looking around, he couldn't make anything out. Everywhere was chaos. Snarling hellhounds thrashed. The lights of their eyes streaked as they jumped around, honing in on their next victim.

He swung at the closest set of eyes, but his aim was off and his attack was weak. The pain in his shoulder was too great to keep fighting. He groaned, falling to the ground.

A scream ran out. Dante snapped back up, adrenaline overtaking his pain. One pair of red eyes was moving away from the group, but it wasn't retreating—it was taking its prize with it.

"Help!" a voice pleaded.

He took off, his legs pumping. With another surge of adrenaline, his shoulder only felt like a dull ache. He wound up his scythe like a baseball bat and swung at the dog with all his might. His arms jarred to a halt as he connected with the beast.

The voice screamed again, and Dante feared he was too late. But the eyes dimmed, and human hands gripped him.

"Thank you, angel," Eva said. Even though it was too dark to see, he still recognized her by her voice.

"I'm no angel," Dante replied.

"You are to me," Eva said firmly.

More screams erupted in the night, but they were cut short with crunching sounds. The sounds of snapping bones.

This is a slaughter. A cold lump sank in his stomach. *I can't save them all.*

But he shook off the sense of dread. He had to save who he could. He focused on another pair of eyes and ran toward them.

A howl escaped from one of the hellhounds. Others joined. It seemed like they were communicating with each other. Snarls and barks filled the darkness. The dogs brushed right past Dante. Their shaggy, mangy fur rubbed against his arms. They didn't pay any attention to him now. The noises became fainter as they left.

His blood pounded in his ears. His scythe was still at the ready. But the hellhounds were leaving. He stood there, dumbfounded. His body was still in fight mode, but the fight had left.

As the silence mounted, he finally understood why they were gone. The hellhounds had eaten their fill.

Chapter 16

Dante was always interested in humans and the human realm. It was so strange to him. He loved accompanying his parents on their various jobs to glimpse what life was like for a human. He couldn't care less about reaping—he knew how that was going to end.

What he really enjoyed were their stories. Humans were a clueless folk. They couldn't understand what life was like after death, but that didn't stop them from coming up with all kinds of ridiculous stories. And even when they were pretty close to the truth, they were still surprised to learn it was real.

But they had stories for everything. Even hope. One story that stuck with him was the story of Pandora's box. In the myth, Pandora opened a box that allowed diseases, envy, hate, and other horrible things to escape into the world. But the last thing that was left in the box was hope.

Why was hope seen as a bad thing? Dante could never understand it. The story always tugged at him, nibbling at the back of his mind. Wasn't hope good to have? After all the suffering, shouldn't you at least have hope for better things to come?

***

Dante stumbled awake as the sun rays streaked across the sky. Even the first few beams of light were hot, warming the cold, hard ground—the ground that was splattered with blood.

He leaped to his feet. The night before rushed back to him like a horror movie playing fast forward. Blinking away the last of his sleep, he realized he must have passed out from exhaustion. His left shoulder seared in pain as it woke up with the blood pounding in his veins. His wounded eye throbbed too, not wanting to be forgotten.

In the morning light, he could see the true damage of the night before. Five people remained: Dante, Sophia, Alex, Eva, and one guy Dante didn't know. Of all the fifteen sinners, only three survived. Eva nursed a wound on her arm. Alex sat on the ground, staring blankly at the sky. The other guy scanned the area as though he was expecting another attack at any moment. He still had a long, pointy rock clasped in his hand.

Only blood was left to show where the other sinners had been. Splatters of red dried and caked on rocks. In a few areas, the blood pooled together. It was still liquid and quivered in the wind. There were no bodies, not even hair left among the rubble. The hellhounds were nothing but thorough. They had eaten them whole.

Dante was a reaper. He was used to seeing death. But not like this. This was a massacre. Chills ran down his spine.

"Hope," Sophia said, her voice wavering. Tears streamed down her cheeks. "This is what hope gets you." She opened her hands, encompassing the slaughter that laid at her feet. "I should have never tried to escape again! It only leads to more suffering!" Her voice that was usually coated with frost now blazed with fury.

"You know why I can't fly?" she screamed in a voice scraped raw. Her eyes were red with tears, and her cheeks flushed with anger. "When I tried to escape before, I flew." She jabbed a finger toward the mountains that rose into the clouds. "I flew up the mountains, beyond the clouds, to Hell's Gate." She paused and pointed. A poignant look crossed her face. "And that's as far as I got."

The memory of seeing her at the gate flashed before Dante's eyes. He still remembered her crying in desperation and gripping his arm. He didn't understand what happened to her that day.

"My father," she started to continue. Her eyebrows tightened, and her lips quivered. "He followed me. He was so furious. He knew I was trying to escape, and he couldn't have that. Not when I was to be his successor." Fresh tears slid down her cheeks, and her voice became quiet and hoarse. "He pulled me back down. I couldn't stop it. I wasn't strong enough. And then—"

Her hands yanked at her hair as if she was trying to pull herself out of her misery.

"He cut my feathers!" she wailed. She fell to her knees, pulling harder at her hair. Her wings opened up, and he saw what she was talking about. At first glance, there didn't appear to be anything wrong with them, but now that they were unfurled, it was obvious. The ends of the feathers were sharp and jagged, crudely chopped.

"So he clipped your feathers like a common house pet?" Alex asked, his face twisting in disgust.

A memory opened in Dante's mind. He was tagging along with his mother to her assignment and followed her into a trailer. The man was sprawled out on the kitchen floor, dead before they even arrived. Empty glass bottles were littered around him with one still gripped in his hand. There was nothing memorable about the man's death except the bird on the counter. The bird squealed and strutted around, fluttering its wings. But no matter how hard it tried, it couldn't fly more than a few feet. At the time, he didn't understand what was wrong with it. *So Sophia is like that bird?*

"I knew I shouldn't have tried to escape again. And now look!" Sophia bowed her head. The spilled blood soaked her white dress as if it stained her with sins. "I have caused these people's deaths. They depended on me, and I couldn't save them. I can't even save myself." Even quieter, she whispered like she was speaking to herself. "I am no better than my father."

A quietness passed between all of them. No one moved. No one spoke.

Dante swallowed a lump in his throat. The more he stared at the blood, the more he heard the screams of pain and the crunching of bones, but he couldn't look away. He was locked in the memories like a living nightmare.

"We need to keep moving."

The voice snapped Dante out of it, pulling him back into the present. It was the other sinner who he didn't know.

"Look," the guy continued. "I know this is a tragedy, but this will happen to us if we don't keep moving. We have to focus on the living now."

In the morning light, Dante could see the guy clearly. His hair was buzzed short, and he had a square jaw with wide shoulders. His eyes were alert, searching for danger.

"What's your name?" Dante asked him.

"Ryan," he answered. He glanced around at the others. "I've been in the military. I've been in combat. I've always thought the battlefield was hell." He paused, thoughtful. "I never knew how right I was. But we don't have a choice. We have to keep fighting."

Dante knew Ryan was right. They had to keep fighting. Or else those people really did die for nothing. And he couldn't let that happen.

"Okay," Dante said. He strapped his scythe on his back and straightened up. "No time to waste."

Alex rose. He still held his sharp rock. He had been unnaturally quiet, but his face spoke volumes. There was a shadow in his eyes. Dante wondered what he had been through. It seemed like the ones who survived were also the ones who had been living in hell long before they came here.

Even Eva had an air of determination about her. She ripped a piece of fabric off the bottom of her robe and wrapped it around her wounded arm. "Yeah, let's go."

Only Sophia still knelt, head bowed. If Dante didn't know any better, he would have thought she was lost in prayer. Who knew, maybe she was. Dante wondered if God heard prayers from Hell.

Slowly, she opened her eyes. He never noticed how clear they were. If he stared too long, he might see her soul gazing back at him.

"You're right," she said, her voice hollow. "We need to keep going." And with that, she stood up. The blood soaked her once white robe. There was something about her that was purified, like she was baptized in it.

He watched her walk away, leaving bloody footprints in her wake. Her wings quivered as she walked. The jagged edges of her feathers cut into his thoughts. *She has already endured so much.*

One feather shook loose and fluttered to the ground. Dante picked it up and inspected it. The feather was crudely chopped. It seemed wrong to leave it here. If they did escape, this feather would still remain like she never truly left.

Everyone was moving on. Without thinking, he shoved it in his inner pocket and hurried after them.

Chapter 17

The rocky ground sloped down gradually as they stumbled past more dead trees. It was slow going. Everyone was nursing wounds and weak from exhaustion. But even more so, the mental anguish of the night before weighed heavily on all of them.

His foot caught on a rock. He flailed, but he couldn't catch himself. He fell, tumbling down the hill. The world spun around him. He came to an abrupt halt when he smacked into a tree. It caught him right in his chest, knocking the wind out of him.

Light floated in front of his eyes. He blinked them away, trying to make sense of what happened. He heard voices, loud and frantic.

"Dante, are you okay?" It sounded feminine, familiar.

Slowly, the pain subsided and the world stopped spinning.

"Yeah," he said. He sat up, groaning. "I'm alive, at least." Wincing, he checked over his body. His chest hurt now—adding to his growing number of wounds—but it didn't seem like he broke any ribs, just bruised them.

Ryan knelt down. "I think we should all rest here. We'll keep getting ourselves hurt if we push too hard."

Dante wasn't going to say no to that. He was beyond exhausted. His arms and legs wouldn't even respond. He flopped down like someone let go of a marionette's strings. Everyone sat down right there on the ground without saying a word. They all were quiet now, trapped in their own private hell.

The silence wasn't really silent when they stopped. At first, Dante heard everyone's breathing, ragged and quick. But soon, their breathing slowed down and the sounds of the wild opened up. Birds cawed, harsh and fierce. Dead leaves rustled in the wind. And in the distance, the sound of running water.

Dante perked up, and so did everyone else.

"Water!" Eva said, snapping up. Light returned to her pale eyes.

They all found the strength they didn't know they had. Dante moved on instinct alone. All his thoughts were focused on getting to the water.

They had to stop a few times to listen where the water was coming from. As they got closer, the sounds of the river became louder. The water sloshed along the riverbanks. Dante reached it first. He knelt at the edge of the river and cupped his hands. The water was murky and gritty, but he gulped it down like it was sweet nectar. It dribbled down his chin as he cupped more water to his lips.

"It's gritty and gross," Eva said, slurping the water out of her palms. "But it's better than nothing."

Alex wiped his mouth. "I don't know about that. I drank sewer water that tastes better than that."

"Ew, really?" Eva laughed.

Alex perked up, evidently happy he made her laugh. "I mean, yeah, this water feels like I'm getting deep-throated by a block of sandpaper."

Eva's mouth snapped closed mid-laugh. "What's wrong with you? Why would you say that?"

Alex grimaced, saying nothing.

She walked away without another word.

By the look on Alex's face, Dante surmised that Alex knew he messed up.

"Whatever," Alex said, kicking a stone.

***

Everyone laid out on the riverbed, needing to rest their weary bones. Scraggly pine trees were scattered along the other side of the river. A few stubborn pine needles held fast on the thin branches, but most of the trees were bare as skeletal remains.

"You know, you can eat bark," Ryan said, eyeing the pine trees.

"What? Ew!" Eva said. She shuddered in disgust.

"How are we supposed to eat bark? Wouldn't we get splinters on our tongues?" Alex asked.

"You have to know which part of the bark you can eat. And some trees are better than others. Pine trees have the best bark." Ryan looked around at everyone's confused faces.

"What are you, the bark connoisseur?" Alex lifted an eyebrow.

"I'll show you," Ryan said, but everyone was quiet. "It's better than starving, right?"

"Sure," said Dante. "It's not like we have any other options."

No one else argued. Ryan led the way, crossing the river toward the trees. The riverbed wasn't deep, only going up to Dante's waist. The pull of the water was strong, but they were all able to cross without any incident, which was a first.

Ryan showed everyone how to remove the bark by using a sharp rock. He shaved off the outer, rough bark off a patch of tree. The gray bark fell away to reveal a greenish layer.

"That's what we're eating?" Eva asked, partly in wonder, partly in distaste.

"Not yet, we still have to scrap past this part," Ryan said as he continued to dig away.

The greenish layer gave way to another. This inner part was a whitish, cream-colored layer.

"This is the part we want," he said. "But be careful. Don't scrap too deep now. We don't want to start carving into the wood of the tree."

"How will we know?" Dante asked, intrigued by the process.

"The bark is softer than the tree wood. You'll feel a difference." He scraped off a piece of the white bark. "Okay, now everyone start. If you don't have something to carve with, then find a sharp rock to use. We need a lot, if we are going to have anything to eat for the rest of the journey."

A journey. *What a choice of words.* It made this whole thing seem so casual, almost normal.

Dante felt refreshed after drinking some water, and so did everyone else. They all got to work. Everyone picked a tree and started scraping off the bark. Dante found himself standing next to Ryan.

"So, did you learn this in the military?" Dante asked.

Ryan laughed and shook his head. "No, I was always interested in survival skills. It was a hobby for me. I would purposely get myself lost in the woods to see if I could find my way back. I learned to get by with a knife or even a sharp rock. And I read a lot of books about what you can and can't eat in the wild." He paused, thoughtful. "I had no idea it would be more useful when I was dead."

Dante paused in his scraping and looked over at him. "How did you die, anyway?"

"A car crash. Can you believe it?" Ryan shook his head again. "Some things you can't prepare for. Like a drunk driver going the wrong way and crashing into you head on."

"Wow," Dante said. "Sorry, that sucks."

"Yeah, but it was instant. No pain, so I guess that's something."

"Yeah," Dante agreed, but his voice was soft. Talking to Ryan reminded him why he was here in the first place. It was so unfair Ryan had to die because some idiot made a really bad decision. So much suffering, and for what?

"So how did a reaper end up in Hell?" Ryan asked with a half smile. "I didn't know that was possible. But I didn't believe any of this was possible."

"Yeah, well, I didn't know either," Dante replied, shrugging.

Ryan chuckled. "So what happened?"

Dante chiseled away at his patch of bark. "I refused to reap anymore. I didn't think it was right to keep sending sinners to Hell."

Ryan was quiet for a moment. Only the scraping sounds filled the air. "I know I'm here for a reason. And I can't even argue about it. I know I deserved it." He looked at Dante. "You shouldn't feel bad about it. You didn't make people sin."

"I get that." Dante sighed. All his thoughts boiled to the surface and spilled out all at once. "But why does it have to happen at all? Why does any of this have to be this way? Why is there Heaven and Hell in the first place? Why does sin even exist? Why do humans have to suffer?"

"Woah, woah, woah, woah," Ryan said. "I can't even begin to answer all that. That's for God to answer."

"Well, I've never met Him to ask."

"You've never met Him?"

"No, reapers aren't even allowed in Heaven. We're too *stained with sin*," Dante sneered.

Fire burned in his blood at the thought. Memories of angels standing back from him, never getting too close as if he was contagious. Memories of angels talking down to him, as if he was beneath them. Angels—they were the real reason he was here. It was a council of angels who decided he was sentenced to Hell, not God.

And Sophia. How did she fit into all of this? Dante glanced in her direction. Since her outburst, she had been quiet, trailing behind them like a ghost with a haunted look on her face. Even now, her head was bowed as she half-heartedly scraped her own section of bark. She did feel remorse for the sinners who died, which was more than he could ever say about any other angel. He still didn't know what to make of her.

Ryan spoke up, interrupting Dante's thoughts. "You know, Jesus is the Son of God, and look what happened to him. Killed by the very people he was trying to help. If he endured such suffering, why would we be any different?"

"Yeah but why suffer at all? What's the purpose of living?" Dante asked, eyebrows furrowing.

"I'm pretty sure that's above my pay-grade." Ryan tried to smile but wiped it away after seeing Dante's face. "Look, I don't know but there's more to all of this than what you see. Why does that make you upset? Isn't it better that there's more to this?"

"Yes, but I want to know what it is."

"The only thing I can say is that whatever is going on, humans are meant to be blind and dumb."

Dante shook his head and made a face. "How can you say that?"

"Think about it. Thomas doubted Jesus to the point where he put his finger in His wounds before he would believe. While demons had no problem knowing who Jesus was and called Him out on it. And all Jesus did was tell them to hush."

Dante paused in his work. "Wait, really?"

"Yes, it's right there in the Bible." Ryan shrugged and laughed ruefully. "Like I said, there's much more to this. And that's all I know." He went back to chopping bark.

Dante stood there, stunned. He wasn't sure what to do with this information.

"Is this good, Ryan?" Eva came around the trunk, holding up a piece of white bark.

"Yeah, that's great. Keep going. We'll need more."

She smiled at him. "Okay."

As she went back to her spot, Dante noticed Alex scowling at Ryan. He was surprised at Alex's reaction. Dante finished getting his chunk of bark off and headed toward Alex.

"Hey," Dante said.

"Hey." Alex answered with a scowl seared on his face. He wasn't scraping bark—he was hacking away at it as if the bark had personally insulted his mother.

"So, how's it going?" Dante asked, eyeing the flying debris.

"Fine." Alex raised his rock and slammed it down into the trunk like he was stabbing it.

"Yeah, it seems like it." Dante raised an eyebrow. He wasn't getting anywhere so he tried a different tactic. "That Ryan guy, huh? He comes out of nowhere, acting like he knows everything."

Alex uttered some profanities.

"What's wrong with him? Seems like a nice guy."

"Yeah, he's *amazing*, isn't he?" The sarcasm dripped from Alex's lips like poison. "Everyone likes him. He knows how to fight, how to survive... *Where would we be without him?*" His voice squeaked higher, impersonating Eva.

Dante's mouth curled up. "Okay...I get that. But why does that make you mad?"

Alex threw his rock down. His hands were raw. "Ryan does everything right. What about me? I haven't done anything to help. I don't know anything useful." He looked up, his eyes bloodshot. "I'm not special like you or Sophia. I'm nobody. Just another sinner in Hell."

"That's not true—"

"Yes, it is! Everything I did was shit when I was alive and here I am again—worthless!" He kicked the ground, stones scattering. "Everyone likes Ryan...No one cares about me."

"I care," Dante said quietly. "You're my friend."

Alex rolled his eyes. "Yeah, whatever." He turned away but stopped. He added, "I never had a friend before."

"Until now."

Alex gave a short laugh and glanced back with a mischievous glint in his eye. "I knew you were a cool reaper."

They shared a smile. Instantly, Dante was transported back to when he first met Alex. *Well, I wondered if Alex could shrug off Hell. It seems like he can.*

Dante clapped a hand on Alex's shoulder. "Come on, don't worry about all that. Let's go enjoy a delicious, gourmet meal." He held up a piece of bark.

Alex groaned. He repeated a few choice words. They were softer this time but they still had an edge to it.

But could Alex shrug off Ryan? Maybe not so much.

Chapter 18

The trees were stripped bare, and the bark was laid out before them.

"It's better if you roast it," Ryan said as everyone tried a piece of bark.

"I can't even eat this," Eva said, frowning. Her piece had chew marks on it but was still intact.

Alex smirked, his rage seething below the surface. "Yeah, so much for all that work we did. This is tougher than jerky."

"Should we risk a fire then?" Dante asked. They could easily collect firewood from all the surrounding trees.

Sophia spat out her bark. "Yes, let's. The hellhounds will find us no matter what. The only good thing is we are hidden in the valley, so no one from the city will see our fire."

Dante wasn't even thinking about that. How easy would it be for the demons to fly over and to swoop them away.

"Oh, so we're still not safe from *them*?" Eva asked, shuddering. Her face scrunched up and a haunted look flashed in her eyes.

Sophia saw Eva's frightened face. "They will only know where we are if we give them a reason to find us," she said soothingly.

Dante noticed Sophia was once again trying to keep Eva calm. Was she still giving her false hope? But he couldn't blame Sophia. Eva seemed easily intimidated and child-like. He couldn't imagine what sin Eva could have possibly committed. She seemed too innocent for that.

"Okay, so let's get firewood before we run out of daylight," Dante said, standing up. Somehow, he still felt like he was the leader. Not sure why, but when he spoke, they listened.

They all began to rise.

"I guess someone knows how to start a fire?" Dante asked it vaguely, but he was looking at Ryan.

Ryan laughed. "Of course I do. And make sure to get some handfuls of dead leaves, too. That will help get the fire going."

"But that will make more smoke," Sophia said. She pursed her lips.

Is she still worried about getting caught?

"Well, then, we'll make sure that it's dark before we start the fire so no one will see the smoke," Dante said.

No one argued that point, so they all got started collecting wood. They split up in different directions but made sure not to go too far away so no one would get lost.

The wind rustled through the trees. The branches groaned and cracked, angry at being disturbed. A few twigs snapped in the wind, scattering across Dante's path like discarded bones. Listlessly dried leaves scurried around.

The sun was setting, and the oncoming cold of dusk was swift. He shivered as he felt the sudden drop of temperature. In the distance, a bird cawed—a shrieking, eerie noise. It didn't sound like any bird he had ever heard before. He glanced around, expecting to see glowing red eyes staring back at him in the shadows. The wind whipped through the trees again, and the air chilled the back of his neck.

A twig snapped to the right of him, and he jumped back in alarm. But it was only Eva. His heart hammered in his ears.

"Oh, I didn't see you," Dante said. He tried to sound casual and not like he almost had a heart attack.

"Sorry," she said. "Is it okay if I stick with you? It's just that..." She trailed off, wringing her hands.

Dante smiled at her. "That's fine. Don't worry about it." He knew after last night, she would be worried to be on her own. It made sense she would come to him. After all, he was the one who saved her. And he didn't think she could hold her own against the hellhounds, unlike the others.

"I haven't had to go get firewood like this since I went camping," she said, leaning down to pick up another stick.

"Did you go camping a lot?" Dante asked. He didn't really care, but it kept his mind off more horrible things.

"Hmm." She shrugged. "Not since my parents divorced."

That didn't give Dante a time reference, but by the way she said it, it sounded like it happened a long time ago.

"Sorry to hear that," he said politely.

"No, it's fine," she said. "They were always arguing. One time they got in an argument about the laundry. Neither one would do the laundry for a month, so I had to Febreze my clothes before school. It was so dumb."

"Oh, really?" He didn't know what to say to that.

"Yeah, and when the basement flooded, they got so mad at each other. It was horrible. My dad ended up punching holes in the wall."

"Oh."

"Yeah, and ...."

She kept talking, but Dante was tuning her out. She didn't seem like a talker, but once she got going, there weren't any signs of stopping. He was getting quite a bundle and would have to turn back to drop them off. He was grateful for it because he hated awkward conversations and it seemed he found one.

"But yeah, it sucked," she said, unaware Dante was inching back away.

He realized he missed a big chunk of conversation, and by the pause, he knew he needed to say something.

"Yeah," he said noncommittally. He cleared his throat. "Hey, we should—"

"But you know what's worse?" she asked, spinning around to face him. It appeared she didn't hear him.

"What's that?" he asked. The pile of wood he was holding was getting heavy and his shoulder ached from where he got bitten. He hoped this was the end of the conversation.

But then he met her eyes. In the shadows, he couldn't see the light of her eyes. They were black and lifeless. A cold wind blew, pricking his skin.

"What's worse was being left alone," she said. Her voice sounded hollow, like it was scraped raw.

As a reaper, Dante was accustomed to people randomly telling him their life stories. But this felt different. This was like a wound that had been left untreated and had festered.

"That must've been hard," he said. For some reason, his heart started beating faster.

"You have no idea. After my parents divorced, I barely ever saw my dad. And my mom was working all the time. Every time I came home from school, I was alone. I had to do homework alone. Eat dinner alone. Watch TV alone. No one to talk to."

Dead leaves crunched as she stepped closer to him. It was hard to see her in the fading light. He wanted to say they needed to turn back, but the words caught in his throat.

"Do you want to know how I died?" Her voice was a whisper, but her words sliced the air.

She held out her hands. Her enlarged veins snaked up her arms. He could barely make out the pinpricks that dotted her skin, but he had seen enough death to know it was from drug use.

"I wanted to feel happy again. To feel something again." A sob caught in her throat. "I didn't mean for it to go so far."

The wind chilled Dante's bones. He didn't know what to say. The silence between them lengthened and stretched between them.

"Dante! Eva!" Ryan called. "You need to come back!" His voice seemed so far away. But it was enough to break the spell that bound Dante in place. He breathed and moved toward the voice.

"We need to go," Dante said. His voice was shaky, and this time, he didn't try to hide it.

He didn't know if she was still in her dark mind-space, but she stayed quiet as they made their way back.

Chapter 19

Ryan struck flint and steel, creating a spark. It quickly spread, thanks to the dead leaves. Smoke billowed into the sky. Up where they couldn't get to. Not yet anyway.

As the fire roared to life, Dante was impressed. "How did you do that?"

"It's not hard, look," Ryan said. Again, he struck the flint with the steel. A little spark flickered. Dante moved closer to see.

Ryan nodded. "I think I found a fellow survivalist. Here, I was able to—*procure*—an extra set of flint and steel." He handed them to Dante.

Dante dropped the pieces in his inner pocket. "Thanks."

Ryan shrugged again as he added another stick to the fire. "It's not a big deal."

Eva side-eyed Ryan. "'Procuring?' Don't tell me you were stealing. You know that's wrong?" She playfully wagged a finger at him.

Ryan grinned. "I don't think stealing from demons counts."

A loud snap made everyone jump. Alex cracked another stick in two. He scowled as everyone focused on him. "What?" he snapped like the branch he just broke. "I'm getting the firewood ready."

"I think we're good now," Ryan said quietly, looking at all the broken sticks scattered on the ground.

Alex harrumphed and threw down the last stick.

***

Soon enough, there were hot coals to cook the bark. Bending down to the fire, Ryan placed the bark strips close to the coals.

"Not too close or you'll burn it," he instructed.

They all followed suit and eagerly watched the bark as it baked.

Dante's stomach growled. He was so hungry even pieces of wood resembled food. At this point, he was willing to eat anything.

"So how long does this take?" Dante asked.

"Not long. Give it some time."

Ryan said it but it didn't make it true. It felt like time slowed down as Dante stared at the only thing even remotely edible in this uninhabitable place.

Finally, Ryan gave them the ok to eat it.

"Ow!" Dante dropped the bark. His fingers still felt the sting.

"It's hot, just so you know," Alex snickered.

"Yeah," Dante grumbled.

He blew on it and this time he was more careful as he tried another bite. It was like thin slices of burnt, crunchy toast.

"Thank you," Dante said to Ryan. "I know we were complaining about the food but really, we would be worse off if you weren't here."

"Are you thanking me for being a sinner so I'm here in Hell?" Ryan asked.

Dante ducked his head. "You know what I mean."

Ryan chuckled.

Then Dante yawned so wide it cracked his jaw. He realized he wasn't the only one. The struggles of the day were finally wearing on everyone. Alex was already lying down while Eva leaned back against a tree. Ryan was still sitting but his hand was propping up his head.

"We should take turns keeping watch," Sophia said.

"What do you mean?" Eva asked.

"We need to watch out for hellhounds, but we also need to rest up for tomorrow. So we will take turns. A few of us to watch and tend the fire while the others sleep."

"That sounds like a plan," Ryan said.

"How are we splitting up, though?" Alex asked.

"How about me and Sophia take the first watch," Dante said, looking to Sophia for approval. She nodded and he continued. "And then, since we have an odd number, it will be the rest of you. No one keeps watch alone."

Dante and Sophia made sure they had enough fuel for the fire while the others stretched out and tried to get comfortable on the hard ground. There were lots of grumbling, but soon enough, the grumblings turned to yawns. Then, it was only the deep breathing of sleep.

Dante and Sophia were quiet, occasionally poking the fire and adding more wood. Sophia seemed to be lost in her thoughts as she gazed into the flames as if they held answers. Dante waited to catch her eye. He had so many questions for her, and here was his chance to ask her, but he didn't know how to breach the subject, or even know where to start.

He finally settled on the question he had been thinking about earlier.

"So what are you going to do when you escape?" Dante asked.

"I don't know," she said, still not tearing her eyes away from the flames.

Dante frowned. "You don't know? You haven't thought about it?"

She was quiet for a few moments. "I don't know if we can even escape at all."

"You think this is impossible?"

"No one has ever actually escaped Hell. As far as I know, I'm the only one to even make it to Hell's Gate."

"What about Lucifer?"

Sophia laughed ruefully, tossing her hair over her shoulder. "I doubt that even crossed his mind. After God sentenced him here, he made it his duty to make a better kingdom than God's. He has it in his head that one day, Hell will rival Heaven in terms of grandeur and power."

He was surprised Lucifer didn't even try to leave, but at the same time, he understood it. What Lucifer was doing was like a big middle finger to God. It was like, "Oh, you're punishing me? Well, I'm going to do it my way and it will be even better!" He liked the appeal of it. Why not remake Hell to be what you wanted? He figured it wasn't a bad idea. If you can't undo the system, why not change it within?

"Don't you think Hell could change?"

She shook her head.

"But why not? Couldn't you change things for the better here? Maybe—"

She laughed again, but this time it was cold and harsh. "You really don't get it, do you?" Her eyes mirrored the flames, orange and bright. "There are things you don't know about this place. It was made for suffering. That's it. Nothing more, nothing less."

She pointed to his left eye that was still bandaged. "That was the first injury you ever got here, wasn't it?"

Dante gently touched his bad eye and got zapped with pain. Blood covered his fingers.

"Have you ever wondered why it hasn't stopped bleeding?" She pressed on, not waiting for an answer. "Your wounds will never heal. The same goes for my wings. My feathers will never grow back."

"And your ankle?" Dante asked, already knowing the answer.

"It will never heal. That's why I deal with the pain. I will have to endure it until either I escape or I die. And that's not the only thing. Notice how everything tastes awful? It's not just because we're eating bark. Even the water, which should be cool and refreshing, is disgusting? In Hell, no thirst can be quenched, no hunger can be satiated. We have tried growing many different kinds of food, but they all taste horrible. Fruit ripe off the vine will sour in your mouth the instant it touches your lips."

Dante remembered how the bread he got that one morning had molded in only a few hours in Hell.

"This place is meant for suffering. And there are more powerful forces in place than my father. There's no changing it," she said. She bowed her head as if the thought was too much to bear.

Something she said nudged a memory out of hiding. *This place is meant for suffering.* It was from the book he found. *This is a place of suffering—a place of ruin and destruction. To think anything different is folly.*

Lost in thought, he tended the fire. The flames rose as he added more wood. The sap popped, expanding in the heat.

He thought about the possibility of not being able to escape. What did that really mean for him? What would he do if he was truly trapped here? His wounds were really starting to add up. Even if he did roam around in Hell, he wouldn't last long before he would be too weak to fight off hellhounds and any other monsters. And then he would surely die.

"What happens when you die in Hell?" he asked.

"Honestly, I don't really know. It's not like people come back to tell you. All I can hope is that it isn't as bad as this place." Her face pinched as if she was willing herself to not cry.

Dante was quiet for a moment. "Can I ask who it was?"

"My mother," she said, wiping her eyes.

A thought occurred to him. *She said her last name was Morningstar.* "Is Cecelia Morningstar your mother?"

"How did you know that?"

"I found a book with her name on it."

"Her journal. I wanted to bring it with me, but it wouldn't have lasted the trip." She shook her head. "She was too good for this place. Yes, she was a fallen angel, but the only sin she committed was believing my father's lies. It's not fair."

They grew silent again, lost in their own thoughts. The snapping of fire was almost peaceful. Dante figured this was the closest he could get to being relaxed. The others were still fast asleep, deeply breathing.

The smoke trailed off to a place where they could only dream of. His eyes followed where his body could not go. Up in the night sky, a moon glowed faintly. It didn't have the blazing heat like the sun, but it shared the same blood red hue.

"My mother used to tell all kinds of stories about angels and Heaven. I loved listening to all of them. And reapers, too." She looked over at him with a half-smile on her face. "I never thought I would meet a reaper, though."

"And I never thought I would meet a fallen angel, but here we are."

"Fair enough." She laughed. It sounded like ringing bells. "Do you remember living in Heaven? What's like there?"

"I've never been there. Reapers were kicked out of Heaven a long time ago, before I was born."

"For what reason?"

"Because reapers are too close to sinners. They were afraid we were tainted. Like we were contagious." A flash of anger made his eyes see red for a moment.

"Hmm, interesting," Sophia said. She put her finger to her chin, apparently oblivious to his burst of outrage. "If they expelled reapers after the Falling happened, I could understand their misgivings. Perhaps they were afraid of more angels defying God." She pointed at him. "Like you did."

He opened his mouth to protest but stopped. *Maybe she does have a point. I never thought of it that way. Maybe that's why The Council was so quick to send me to Hell. They might've been afraid of another rebellion on their hands.*

"So when they expelled the reapers out of Heaven, was that when they took their wings, too? Is that why?"

"What are you talking about?"

"They were stories when I was child, but it is said reapers once were angels, wings and all."

Dante scoffed at that ridiculous notion. The mere thought made him recoil. "I'm not an angel, that's for sure."

Sophia stared at him, her eyes wide. "So you don't know reapers were once called 'angels of death'?"

"I never heard that."

He touched his shoulder blades. Nothing was there to indicate there could be wings. He paused for a moment, thinking.

"So I'm technically an angel who was also cast out of heaven? So we're the same?"

Sophia scrunched her face. "I wouldn't go that far. Remember, I didn't do anything wrong." It sounded accusing but she smiled as she said it.

Dante grinned.

"Say we do get out of here. Just for a moment, entertain the idea," Dante said as Sophia pursed her lips.

She sighed. "Okay, fine. For a moment, I'll pretend this could happen."

"What would you do? And you have to really think about it this time."

She paused, thinking.

"I promised my mother I would enter Heaven one day, for her sake and mine. The real challenge would be to know if the other angels would even accept me. The thing is, I'm not one of the original Fallen. I was never banished to this place. I was born here, through no fault of my own. But a part of me fears they will still turn their backs on me." She frowned. "What if I'm not allowed in Heaven?"

Her words left a hole in his heart. *I guess we are more similar than I realized.*

"So what?" he said with a wicked grin.

"What do you mean?"

"Who cares if the other angels don't like you?" he asked, shrugging. "None of them liked me, either. We can break into Heaven instead."

"You can do that?"

"If we can escape Hell, what can't we do? I've never been allowed into Heaven. I want to see what all the fuss is about. What do you say? Would you come and break into Heaven with me?"

She laughed—a pure laugh that came right from the heart. "Why is it that you give me hope when before I had none?"

"So is that a yes?"

A smile spread across her face and brightened up her eyes. "Yes."

Dante laughed and she did, too.

There was something in the air—the air of possibility. In the dead of the night, in the pit of Hell, there was hope. It was a single flicker of flame in the dark, but they latched onto it.

And together, they might just make it work.

Chapter 20

He woke up to something burning. His heart seized as he sprang up.

"You want some bark bacon?" Alex asked. He smirked as he held up a burnt piece of wood under Dante's nose.

Dante let out a sigh of relief, trying to calm his heart down. "Oh, yeah, how did you know that was my favorite?" he asked, swiping it from Alex's hand.

Alex laughed. "I had to wake you up somehow, sleepyhead. Everyone else has been awake for a while, and we have to get going soon."

Sure enough, the sun was already climbing the sky. The heat was gathering fast. Sweat formed on his brow.

He looked down at the charcoal chunk in his hand. "I get the burnt piece, huh?"

"The early bird catches the worm," Alex teased. "And sleepyheads get the burnt pieces. But I guarantee it tastes the same."

Dante broke off a piece with his teeth. It tasted like crunchy smoke. "Delicious," he choked out.

Alex smiled. "I guess you feel better today."

Dante gulped. The paste scraped his throat on the way down. "Of course. Today, we can climb the mountain. And then get the hell out of here." His eyes found Sophia. "Right, Sophia?"

She nodded. "Yes, the mountains are the last obstacle. Once we are up the mountain, we will be at Hell's Gate."

"So what are we waiting for?" Ryan jumped up and started gathering the pieces of bark and stuffing them into his pockets.

"What do you need me to do?" Eva asked, running up to him.

"Here, help me get water to put out the embers," he said.

She eagerly began assisting him. She leaned in close, their skin touching.

"Hmph."

Dante turned back to Alex, whose mouth slid into a frown. The seething rage from the day before was back. Dante thought Alex just didn't like Ryan, but it seemed there was more to it.

"What's wrong?" Dante asked, but he knew the answer. *I think he likes her, too.*

Alex's face twisted in a grimace. "I don't know why she's so eager to please Ryan. He acts like he knows everything. What did he really do, anyway? He made us eat bark and start a fire. Big deal."

Dante's eyes scrunched up at Alex's words. He remembered a different tone yesterday. *Ryan does everything right...I don't know anything useful...I'm not special.* His sarcasm was a shield to guard his true feelings. But Dante could see right through it.

"Look, you have good qualities too," Dante said.

"Huh? What're you talking about?"

"Just give Eva time to see it too."

Alex scoffed and looked away. "I'm nothing like Ryan."

"Dante! Alex! Let's go," Sophia called, waving them on. The rest of them were already waiting to go up the slope toward the mountain.

Alex sulked away.

Dante felt bad but he wasn't sure what to say. He sighed and joined everyone else.

"Is everyone ready?" Ryan asked when they were all gathered together.

"As ready as I'll ever be," Sophia replied. Her fingers turned to fists.

"We just gotta make it up the mountain," Dante said.

Alex squinted as he tilted his head back to see the full scale of the mountains. "Oh, is that all?"

Dante glanced over at him, trying to see if he was still upset, but Alex wouldn't look at him or anyone.

Without another word, they began their journey up the mountain.

***

Scraggy dead trees dotted the mountain. Every time the wind blew, the branches creaked and groaned. In the distance, a bird cawed. The only other sound was the crunching of rocks beneath their feet while they scaled the rocky mountainside.

Climbing made his heart rate increase and more blood pump to his injuries. Warm liquid flowed down his cheek and down his arm.

"Are you okay?" Sophia asked. Her eyes followed the trail of blood Dante was leaving behind.

Dante's breath was harsh and ragged. *What if I really do die before I can escape? What will happen to me then?*

"I'm fine," he said. What else could he say? They had already lost time yesterday gathering food and making a fire. It wouldn't help anyone to make them stop for him when they really needed to keep climbing the mountain.

He crouched down and tore another strip off the bottom of his robe. He wrapped it around the bite marks on his shoulder and tightened the other cloth around his head. It wouldn't stop the bleeding, but it was the only thing he could do right now.

"Are you sure?" Sophia asked, doubt clouding her eyes.

Dante knew she was thinking of their conversation last night. Under the stars, everything seemed so simple. But in the harsh sun, those hopes of escaping and breaking into Heaven seemed to vanish like the smoke from their fire. He didn't want to feed her growing doubt that this was a fool's journey.

He tried to smile but he felt his face grimace instead. "Yeah, come on, no time to lose."

She frowned but said no more.

The boulders were now so big they had to help each other climb up. Dante noticed Alex was too eager to help Eva and elbowed Ryan out of the way.

"Woah!" Ryan fell forward. He caught himself on a protruding rock, sending a cascade of stones down the rough terrain.

A cold hand squeezed Dante's heart as he realized Alex was taking this crush thing too far. *Maybe I should've tried to talk him out of it.*

He climbed up the rock next to Alex, trying not to notice he was leaving bloody handprints in his wake.

"Hey Alex, can you help me up?" he asked.

Alex was already turning to go help Eva, but he begrudgingly spun back to Dante. His eyes softened when he saw how much blood Dante was losing.

"Seriously, man, are you okay?" Alex asked.

"I'll be alright." Dante let Alex give him a hand up another steep boulder. He purposely took his time in order to separate them from the others.

"I know you like Eva," Dante began, lowering his voice, "but it doesn't seem like Ryan likes her. I don't think you have anything to worry about." He wasn't sure if Eva liked Alex either, but he wasn't going down that road.

Alex's face scrunched up. "But Eva likes Ryan."

"Are you sure?" Dante didn't get that impression, but then again, he didn't know much about human girls.

"Are you kidding me? Why do you think she's always finding reasons to talk to him?"

"Mmm, maybe." Dante still wasn't convinced. He figured it was jealousy talking. "But still, we need everyone to work together if we want to get out of here. Right?" He looked pointedly at Alex.

Alex scowled. "Yeah, whatever." He turned away and climbed up the next boulder himself, not bothering to help Dante.

Dante watched him go, distance widening between them.

***

He groaned as he pulled himself up another boulder. He realized he was the weak link in the group. But it seemed they had no problem going on without him. Apparently, the closer they got to their goal, the more out for themselves they were. Maybe they weren't ever a cohesive group to begin with.

A loud squawk made him jump. Whipping his head around, he saw a murder of crows flying in the sky, not far from him. The sight of them made him shudder and shrink into the rocks.

Then he heard the others. They were only a good stone's throw away.

"Hey!" he called, raising his voice to be heard. Even though he was sure he spoke loud enough, it didn't seem like they heard him. They were arguing, but he could only pick up pieces of what was being said.

"We need to help each other," Sophia was saying as Dante climbed the last rock.

"What does it matter? We know what to do. We just need to climb this mountain and then we're out of here," Alex said.

"It's not that simple," Sophia said. Her lips pursed together. It seemed like they had been arguing for a while now.

"Hey, I'm all for helping people," Ryan said. "It's Alex here who is the problem. He nearly pushed me off the cliff."

Alex rounded on him. "Shut up! You don't know what you're talking about."

Ryan put his hands up. "Hey, I'm not trying to start a fight. You need to chill."

"Stop telling me what to do."

Eva covered her ears. "Guys, please stop fighting."

"Humans!" Sophia huffed. She spotted Dante first. "Can you talk some sense into them?"

Dante sighed. It didn't go well the last time he tried talking to Alex. And now emotions were even more heated.

"Look," Dante said, meeting everyone's eyes. Alex looked away. "We are wasting time. We need to get to the top of the mountain before dark." Dante pointed to the sun. "It's already afternoon. And we are not even halfway yet. That doesn't include what is beyond the clouds." He tried to keep his voice steady and pretended to not notice the blood dripping down his arm. *If I even make it that far.*

Maybe it was his words, or maybe it was the blood, but either way, they grew quiet. The silence hung heavy with emotions, but he felt it was progress.

"So let's keep going," he said, trying to keep them focused before it all fell apart again. He didn't wait for them to start climbing. Sophia came next, close behind. He didn't check to see if the others were following. At this point, he didn't care. He was so tired. His muscles ached and his wounds throbbed in pain. His head felt light from the loss of blood. He didn't have any energy left to babysit people's tantrums, too.

Then a scream pierced the air.

Chapter 21

"Help!" Ryan dangled by one hand. His feet kicked nothing but air.

"Hold on!" Dante shouted.

Ryan tried to grab the rock with his other hand, but it slipped, sending small stones scattering far below him.

Dante desperately scanned the area for a solution, but there was no way for him to get to Ryan fast enough. He locked eyes with Alex, who was the closest to Ryan.

"Alex!" Dante said. "Go help him!"

Alex was in the middle of helping Eva up. *Of course he is.*

"Go!" Dante shouted. His heart knocked against his chest.

"I'm going!" Alex shouted back. He shuffled closer to Ryan.

Dante watched helplessly. He gripped the rock beneath him, turning his knuckles white.

Ryan held on with one hand as if he was hanging by a thread. One strong wind could knock him right over.

Alex climbed over a rock, inching closer to Ryan. Every step looked like he was treading water.

Dante snapped, "Hurry up!" His heart was in his throat.

Alex grabbed Ryan's arm.

Dante allowed himself to breathe.

Ryan swung his other arm up and Alex reached for it. But as Alex adjusted his weight so he could pull Ryan up, he slid on the rocks. Alex fell forward and Ryan's grasp slipped.

Ryan fell. Screaming, he plummeted down the mountain.

"No!" Dante barely recognized his own voice—a hollow, horrified sound. All he could do was watch Ryan's body spin in the air. He was so small and insignificant against the magnitude of the mountain.

And then everything stopped. Ryan's body was sprawled out on jagged rocks, far below him.

"Ryan!" Dante yelled.

"Dante," Sophia said quietly. "It's too late."

He couldn't accept that. He scrambled down toward Ryan. As he half-climbed, half-slid down, he vaguely heard Eva crying and Alex saying, "It wasn't my fault," over and over again. He wasn't sure if Alex was telling him that or himself. At the moment, Dante didn't care.

Stones clattered around him as he slid down to Ryan. Dante's eyes locked on him the entire way down, but Ryan hadn't moved. Dante's head spun. He didn't want to believe it.

Ryan had fallen on his back with his limbs sprawled out and his neck at an odd angle. Even though Dante had seen death many times, he wasn't prepared for this. He plodded down on the ground next to him with a heavy heart. Ryan's eyes were glazed over. The light was gone from them.

Dante's throat tightened. He was sentenced to this place because he didn't want to be a part of any more needless suffering. And yet, here he was, still a part of all this misery. But all he could do was watch. Nothing had changed. Except now, he was useless, even as a reaper. His scythe weighed heavily on his back. There was no need for that here.

"I'm sorry, Ryan," he said. "I'm sorry for everything." Dante felt responsible for his death. If it wasn't for Dante, Ryan wouldn't have been here at all. *And after all he did for us.* Dante bowed his head.

A soft wind blew, rippling his robe. Flies buzzed. The sun soaked the ground with its rays. Time passed, but Dante didn't want to leave. It felt wrong to leave him here, like he was abandoning him.

Stones shifted above him. He looked up through tears threatening to release themselves. Sophia was making her way down to him.

"What are you doing?" he choked out. "Shouldn't you be getting to the top of the mountain by now?"

"Don't be stupid," Sophia said. Her eyes glistened with tears. "I couldn't leave you here."

Dante bowed his head again, emotions welling up in him.

Sophia came and kneeled next to him. She whispered a prayer. He couldn't understand the language she spoke, but the sounds were pure and calming.

He had never been one for praying, but he said a silent prayer for Ryan's soul. *Please have mercy. I don't know what he did to deserve this place, but he's been nothing but helpful and kind. Please bring him to a better place.*

A peaceful silence followed. They stayed like that for some time.

"You really do care," Sophia said quietly.

"What do you mean?"

"About the sinners. You really care about them. When you said you were sent to Hell because you couldn't send sinners here anymore, I wasn't sure if that was the real reason." She met his eyes and smiled through the tears. "But you really do care."

"So do you," he said. "I never met an angel who truly cared about sinners."

"You know what? I think when we get out of here and break into Heaven, I think God is going to have to answer a lot of questions."

"You still think we'll be able to do that?"

"Definitely."

Even though her robe was stained and her hair was matted, she was so beautiful. The sun beamed around her as if she glowed.

Her gaze turned from him and she gasped. Ryan's body was gone. He had simply vanished.

"What happened?" Dante glanced around like he expected to see Ryan walking around.

"I think our prayers were answered."

"I hope so." *And if so, does that mean God can hear us? Does that mean we aren't completely abandoned?* More questions but never any answers.

He met Alex's gaze. Alex did reach Ryan and tried to help him up. But what if he didn't linger and got to Ryan sooner? Maybe then he could have saved him. Dante replayed those moments over and over in his head, but he couldn't decide if Alex was really at fault or not. Was he really being slow or was it Dante's perception? At the same time, he couldn't really look at him the same way.

Sophia put her hand on his shoulder. "I think it's time. We need to go now. You know Ryan would have wanted the same," she said.

Dante nodded. They started their journey back up the mountain.

***

By the time they reached the others, the sun had sunk lower in the sky. It was late afternoon. The shadows were getting longer and the wind was chilly.

Sophia and Dante sat down, breathing heavily. His legs shook. His arms ached and were caked with blood. But most of all, his stomach growled. He hadn't eaten anything since this morning.

Alex held out a piece of bark to Dante. Dante stared at it and then at Alex. A lot had changed since the last time Alex gave him a piece. A silence passed between them.

"Come on," Alex said. "I know you're hungry."

Dante frowned, feeling the pull of opposing thoughts in his head. He really thought of Alex as his friend. But was it really Alex's fault? Dante's heart ripped at the seams.

Dante hesitantly took the bark. It felt like a betrayal to Ryan.

A heavy silence loomed over them like rain clouds. They all were lost in their thoughts, not even meeting each other's eyes.

"It wasn't my fault," Alex declared.

"You were the only one who could help Ryan," Dante said.

Alex threw up his arms. "I tried to help him! You saw me."

Dante frowned, thinking. The memories kept going round and round. He wasn't sure what to believe.

Alex sighed in frustration and rounded on Eva. "You saw me, right?"

"Yeah," Eva answered. She didn't seem sure.

"Don't tell me you think it's my fault, too!"

At his outburst, she shrank into herself.

Alex got up and paced back and forth. His hands curled to fists. "I can't believe everyone thinks it's my fault!"

Sophia sighed. "Playing the blame game isn't helping anyone. What is done is done. We really should get going."

Alex rounded on her. "Are you sure? Do you want to let a murderer out of Hell?"

Dante grimaced. "Hey, no one is saying you killed Ryan."

"I wasn't talking about Ryan," Alex snapped. He let his words sink in.

"Wait, what?" Dante stuttered.

"You heard me. I got tired of my dad beating my ass. I found his old shotgun. Did some target practice." Alex crossed his arms. "So, go ahead and judge me. I don't give a shit." He turned away from them and began climbing the mountain.

Dante sat there, stunned. He knew Alex was here for a reason, but for murder? And his own father? He watched Alex go up the rocks. *Do I really want him to escape Hell? Escape his punishment?*

It wasn't fair. Alex would get to escape and Ryan couldn't. Dante glanced down over the cliff, still seeing Ryan's body in his mind's eye. And what happened to him? Wherever he was, Dante hoped he was in a better place. If their prayers really were answered, then that would truly be a blessing.

"Are you coming, Dante?" Eva asked. Her eyes were red from crying.

Dante felt a pang of sympathy. None of this was her fault. He gave her a small smile to show no hard feelings.

A strong wind blew past him, threatening to push him off. Dante clung to the rocks. In the corner of his eye, he saw a strange dark cloud. It was going against the wind.

And it was headed straight toward them.

Chapter 22

The black cloud was coming fast. As it approached, he noticed black wings flapping. But this time it wasn't a murder of crows. His blood froze—they were demons.

There was no way he could put up a fight. There were too many of them. He shouted to Sophia. Even though there was quite a distance between them, he could read the expression on her face clearly. It was the face of defeat.

With wild shrieks, the demons descended upon them like vultures. One demon with fangs and yellow eyes swooped toward him. Dante didn't have any energy left to fight. But he faced the demon head on, steeling himself for the inevitable death.

The demon flew toward him, talons out. And yanked him off his feet. The ground fell away as he was carried up into the sky. The other demons scooped up Sophia, Eva, and Alex. They all dangled in the air while the demons grasped them by their shoulders.

With another screech, the demons whisked them away. Apparently, they had no intention of killing them. Not yet, anyway.

Instead, they were flying right back to the city. Like he never left at all. Heat boiled in his veins. No matter what he did, it didn't matter. Lucifer's words whispered in his ear: *Everything you do is for nothing. You are nothing.* What was the point of trying? Why have hope?

Questions with no answers. That's all he had. There was nothing he could do but watch as the demons led them to the last place Dante wanted to be.

***

Out of all the distance they traveled, walked, stumbled, climbed—so much time and energy, so much sweat, blood, and tears—they weren't really that far from the City of Dis. They came upon the city in no time. What fate awaited Dante back at the city, he didn't know, but there was no way it could be good.

They arrived at the city, but really, it was just smoking ruins. The ground was cracked into spiderwebs from the intense heat and earthquakes. The cinders were still hot, and the smoke rolled across the huge flattened blackened area. Looking at the city from above, Dante saw how expansive it really was.

Wings dipped down as they descended. Sinners were toiling away in the wreckage while demons stood over them with cracking whips. Screams of pain whistled in his ears as they breezed right past them. *Where are we going?*

It was one question that did have an answer. In the center of the smoke and ruins was Lucifer, shining bright against the rubble.

Here, the demons landed and dumped them unceremoniously on the ground. Dante fell, inhaling ashes. Coughing, he glanced at the others. They didn't look any better than Dante felt. Eva's face was streaked with tears. Alex kept his eyes down and his face was in a permanent scowl. And Sophia was the worst out of them all. Her once golden hair dimmed to a pale yellow. There were no tears in her eyes but her whole face and shoulders sagged with an invisible weight. Even her wings were limp and drooped on her back.

Lucifer smirked at their sorry state. He opened his arms and proclaimed, "Today is a new day. I will build a better city, one to rival the Kingdom of God. This time, I will have the perfect city to rule over. One that will outshine the glory of God, one that will never fall to ruins. I will create the world how I want."

Lucifer stared in front of him, but his eyes glazed over as if he were caught in a daydream. "Mine will be better," he whispered earnestly.

He's still bitter about being thrown out of Heaven. He can't let it go. Am I the same? He shuddered at the thought. *When Lucifer talks like that, he sounds like a bratty child. Do I sound like that? Am I too arrogant to think I know better?*

The demons pushed Sophia toward Lucifer. She looked so pitifully small against the huge, scaly demons.

"Sophia." Dante's voice cracked. Out of everyone here, he felt like he let her down the most. Not only did he promise they would escape, but they would break into Heaven, too.

"Sophia is my daughter. She will no longer converse with a lowly reaper. Go be with the sinners you love so much," Lucifer sneered, waving his hand at Dante as if wishing for him to disappear.

"She doesn't want to be here!" Dante hands tightened to fists. A demon held him back.

"Dante, don't," Sophia said softly. She didn't meet his eyes.

At her words, he faltered. This was truly the end of their escape. Everything had completely fallen apart.

Lucifer had been silent, watching their exchange. Now he chuckled as if there was something funny.

"What did I tell you when you got here, reaper?" he asked. He smiled, revealing his pearly white teeth.

Dante stared at him but said nothing.

"I guess you need a reminder then." Lucifer was undeterred. His golden eyes gleamed. "I told you everything you do was for nothing. You are nothing." He emphasized the last three words, letting them hang in the air.

"Do you believe me yet?" Lucifer whispered.

Dante gulped, feeling a lump grow in his throat. Hot tears threatened to spill over, but he refused to let Lucifer see. He quickly blinked them back.

But Dante's silence told Lucifer all he needed to hear. Lucifer's smile widened even more—a jagged, unnatural smile.

"You do realize I knew you were trying to escape the whole time. I sent my spies to keep an eye on you." Lucifer pointed to the sky.

Circling the air was the murder of crows. They swooped and cawed. He had seen them while they climbed the mountain. His stomach sank. They never had a chance.

"Throughout the years, I realized the best way to completely break someone's spirit was to give them hope," Lucifer continued.

Dante turned his attention back to Lucifer and met his cruel eyes.

"Nothing is worse than almost getting everything you want and then having it snatched away from you at the very end. Don't you agree?"

Dante hung his head, not saying a word. There was nothing to say. Everything was ruined.

Lucifer laughed—a cruel, wicked laugh. He gestured at the demons. "Send them away."

"What will you have us do with them?" the demon behind Dante asked.

"Alastor, take them to the fields. You know what to do."

Alastor tightened his grip on Dante. "Yes, Light-Bringer."

Lucifer addressed Dante. "Go ahead and plan your escape again. Maybe you'll make it farther next time before we pluck you back."

The demons cackled.

Dante had taunted Lucifer the first time they met. He wasn't in that kind of position anymore.

Lucifer grabbed Sophia by the arm. "We have a lot of work to do."

Sophia turned toward Dante, tears filling her eyes. "I'm sorry."

"You have nothing to apologize for," Dante said.

Alastor took flight, taking Dante with him. Two other demons followed with Eva and Alex. Alastor flew to a field on the far side of the city, beyond the walls. It was a wheat field, a sea of grain. It felt endless. It was sprinkled with ash, but overall, the destruction of the city didn't affect it.

"So what am I doing?" Dante asked glumly.

"You are a reaper," Alastor said. "Go reap."

Chapter 23

The sun was blazing. It was so intense it felt like hot coals on his face. Sweat trickled down his back.

Yes, I am a reaper. With a sigh, he swiped his blade across the stalks. The fallen grain laid dead in his wake. Before him, the stalks stood tall, blissfully unaware of their imminent demise.

All he had were thoughts to fill his mind. His arms swung mindlessly in front of him. He hacked away at the sea of grain, one drop at a time.

Hope. There was no hope. Only a fool's hope. Only a flicker of light in the dark that was quickly snuffed out, smothered by the overwhelming force of nothingness.

Maybe Lucifer is right. None of this even mattered. Everything I did was for nothing. He swung his scythe, sweeping the blade, watching the grain fall. *How could I ever escape Hell? I can't even escape the purpose for which I was created.* Even in Hell, Dante couldn't escape his fate of who he was. How ironic. *Maybe this is my own personal hell. I will always be stuck being a reaper.*

As more stalks fell, he only saw Ryan falling to his death. The moment played over and over again in his head. All he could see was Ryan desperately clinging to the rock, his feet dangling in the air. Dante could only watch in horror as Ryan fell until his body crashed on the rocks below.

His chest tightened. The memory crashed into him, making it hard to breathe. It was the first time Dante felt truly helpless. He could do nothing for Ryan. He couldn't reap his soul and lead him to the otherside. Dante had always taken that ability for granted. And now, even that was gone.

The whip cracked. His back lit up like fire, burning flesh. He cried out in pain. Blinking, he didn't realize he had stopped. He was just standing there with his scythe in his hands.

"Get back to work!" Alastor shouted.

The whip cracked in the air again as a warning. Stiffly, he swung his weapon again, hacking at the wheat. His back screamed in agony. He squinted in the hot sun, making his wounded eye ache. He remembered what Sophia said. *No wounds will heal.* Every injury he endured, he would endure forever.

Why am I even trying? It was only a fool's hope to think I could ever escape. Now I know the truth. If I try to escape, Lucifer and his minions will fly and bring me back here. And that's the best case scenario. They could get tired of that and decide to torture me for the rest of eternity.

Hours in the hot sun. Hours of sending more grain to their deaths. After a long time, the sun began to sink behind the mountains—the very mountains he had climbed this morning. But now the shadows were stretching across the land. Dante's own dark shadow billowed out like the black robe he wore. His scythe's black mirror image appeared in the fallen grain.

It was all a fool's hope. Dante stared at his shadow. *I can't escape. Not anymore.*

***

In the late afternoon, the sun was at its hottest. Sweat dripped down Dante's forehead and gathered at the base of his neck. His arms and back ached from swinging his scythe. The grain behind him laid bare, sad, and dejected.

Sinners appeared like gray ghosts. They shuffled through fallen grain and scooped it up. While the demons watched with yellow eyes, they loaded it on a wooden wagon. Soon the grain rose in a huge heap and the ground was barren. The stubble of stalks was the only thing left to show grain once stood there.

"That's enough for today, reaper," Alastor said. He spat out *"reaper"* like it was an insult.

Great, I get shit on by angels and now demons. He dropped his scythe—he couldn't bear to hold it anymore.

Once they were done loading the grain into the wagon, the sinners pulled the wagon as if they were beasts of burden. Dante stood there dumbly, not knowing what to do.

"Pick up your scythe and follow," Alastor said over his shoulder.

Dante sighed and bent down to pick it up. It laid among the remaining scattered stalks. The blade was dull and lifeless. No light touched it. The scythe felt like dead weight in his hands, a burden and reminder of why he was here—and who he was. The fate he couldn't escape.

He stared at the scythe. The very same scythe the old reaper gave him. That felt like a lifetime ago, like it happened to someone else. When the old man said one day Dante would get his real scythe, he didn't think much of it, but now, he couldn't help but to think there was more to it. *Isn't that what Ryan said? How there's more to this than we ever could know? Is he right? Are we supposed to be blind? But I want to know.*

The demons led Dante and the sinners to their pitiful shack, where they were to rest for the night. Their whips hovered close. They allowed them to rest but the message was clear: They were still trapped.

Dante lay down on the dirt floor, staring up at the rotting wood beams. It was a small relief from the sun and its unforgivable heat. The stale air felt cold compared to the outside. A single candle flickered and sputtered, throwing up long, ever-changing shadows on the walls and roof. Outside, the wind howled. It screamed and shook the shack. Oddly enough, it didn't feel much different from his reaper home. *What does that say about how I lived?*

He quietly ate his bread that was his payment for the day. It was dry and tasteless, but he ate it without complaint. The other sinners were talking around him, but he ignored them. He was glad to not be in the fields, endlessly harvesting wheat.

"What do you got in your pocket?" a rough voice asked.

"None of your business," a very familiar voice sneered.

"You better not be hiding anything from me," the rough voice said.

Alex was talking with an older man. The man's hair was shaggy and haphazard. He had squinty eyes and his pot belly stretched out the front of his robe.

"I told you, I don't have anything," Alex said.

From Dante's perspective, he saw Alex slide his hand behind his back. He was definitely hiding something.

"Don't you lie to me, boy," the man said, shaking a fist. "I saw you. Now turn out your pockets!"

Alex cleverly hid the item in the belt of his robe. He then complied and turned his pockets inside out.

"See, I told you I didn't have anything," Alex said.

The old man frowned, wrinkling his face like a prune. "You had something, I know it. I saw you eating something."

Alex cocked his head to the side. "Yeah, I was. That yucky bread they gave us."

"No, I smelled something different. It smelled like burnt wood."

Dante focused on what was tucked in Alex's belt. Yes, it was a piece of bark. Somehow Alex still had some.

"Yeah, well, they burnt the bread. I don't know what else to tell you," Alex said, shrugging.

Dante looked curiously between them. The way they talked and interacted—it seemed like they knew each other. Like this scenario has happened many times before.

"You lie! You're always lying!" the man said, his voice rising. "Haven't I raised you better?"

So they did know each other. *Is this Alex's father? The one he shot and killed?*

The man shoved Alex, making him stumble and fall. The whole shack shook.

"Raised me better? How would you even know—you were always drunk!" Alex shot back while he stood up.

"I put a roof over your head. I gave you food. I put the clothes on your back. And this is the thanks I get."

"Oh, sorry, I guess I forgot since you came home late at night, if you even came home at all. I was lucky if you passed out on the front lawn instead of at the police station."

"You ungrateful brat!"

"You drunk asshole!"

The man threw Alex against the wall. "I'll teach you some manners!"

Dante stood up, pulling out his scythe. "That's enough." He pointed the blade at the old man.

"Hey, you're a reaper!" the man sputtered. He backed away.

"Dante, I don't need your help," Alex said.

Dante frowned and put his scythe back. Without another word, he sat back down. Alex and his father continued bickering but Dante shut it out. It wasn't that hard to. He was so tired he fell asleep as soon as he closed his eyes.

***

He woke up to the smell of burnt wood. Again.

"Wait, what?" Dante asked, blinking sleep out of his eyes.

"Shh," Alex said. He held up a piece of bark. "Eat it quickly before my dad wakes up."

Dante realized it was morning. The sun peeked through the cracks in the roof, trying to get in. Dust motes danced in the light as the deep breathing of slumber blew them around.

He studied the bark. It was smaller than the piece Alex hid from his father. Alex was already eating the supposed other half.

The night before flashed before his eyes. *You lie! You're always lying!* The voice rang in his head. Alex's dad seemed to have a drinking problem, but that didn't diminish his ability to know when Alex was lying. Because he *was* lying. Dante saw how sneaky Alex was. *What else has Alex lied about?* Dante still couldn't look at him the same after Ryan died. He didn't know exactly what he saw. And Alex said he tried to help Ryan. *But was he lying?*

"So that's your dad, huh?" Dante asked. He swallowed the smushed bark paste in his mouth.

"Yeah, what you saw was every day of my life." Alex scowled. "And now I have to deal with it again, even after I'm dead. This really is Hell."

A few of the others stirred. Dante and Alex held their breaths, trying not to wake them. He didn't know how much longer they had until the demons came for them.

"But he doesn't know, does he?" Dante didn't know how to really ask the question, but he figured if Alex was having an argument with his father, wouldn't it be about getting killed and not about hiding food?

Alex gave Dante a hard look—one that Dante had never seen before. The glint in his eyes was made of steel.

"You think I'm that stupid? I waited until he was drunk enough to pass out. I didn't have to wait long." Alex held his gaze. "And you better not breathe a word to him." The tone had a hint of threat, not unlike how Alex's father had talked last night.

Dante's stomach turned sour. He thought of Alex as his friend, but now it seemed like Alex was showing his true colors. Could he really be trusted?

A silence passed between them. One of the sinners snored lightly while demons shuffled outside.

Alex sighed and rubbed his forehead. "I bet you think I'm a bad person now. That I deserve all this." He hung his head, dejected.

Dante couldn't exactly disagree with him.

"Look," Alex said. "I know what I did was wrong. But I couldn't see any other way. I couldn't watch my mom and little brother getting beat up any more. I had enough. I had to make sure he couldn't hurt them ever again."

Dante opened his mouth to ask another question that had been hanging on his mind, but a demon slammed open the door. The others woke up with a start.

"Get up! Time to work." The demon flicked his eyes around the room. His eyes landed on Dante. "And you're coming with me."

Dante sighed, already feeling weary even though he just woke up.

"Well, see you later," he said.

"Yeah," Alex replied glumly, looking over at his father. The old man squinted, frowning.

Dante could already feel the next argument brewing.

"Hurry up," the demon snapped at Dante. He pushed Dante out of the shack.

Blinking in the harsh light, Dante surveyed the endless grain. *Another day of harvesting wheat. Is this what my life will be like all day, every day? For eternity?* Hopelessness filled his entire body.

A whip cracked and sear of pain bolted through his shoulders.

"I said, hurry up!"

With a heavy sigh, Dante grabbed his scythe off his back. *Here we go again.*

Chapter 24

The shadows lengthened. Wheels creaked. Another day was done. The sinners with the wagon came to load up the grain.

Dante lowered his scythe, panting. His arms trembled. He never wanted to see another grain of wheat again.

He spotted Eva among the other sinners. He hadn't seen her since the demons took them away.

"Hey, Eva," he said. His voice croaked from the lack of water.

She glanced at him before turning her attention back to her job.

A few moments paused and he realized she wasn't going to talk to him.

"Eva, what's wrong?"

A few more minutes passed. He watched her load up the grain into the wagon. But before he turned away, she finally spoke.

"It's really over, isn't it?"

He stopped. "What do you mean?"

Her eyes were full of tears. She looked mournfully at him. "It's all over—everything. There is no escape from this place, is there?"

His heart sank. He didn't know what to say. He only knew she was right. And somehow, he felt like they were worse off than they were before. Because before they had hope. And now they had none.

***

Dante returned to the shack. Alex bursted out the door with his father close behind him.

"Get back here, boy!" he yelled with raised fists.

"I'm already in Hell. I'm not spending eternity with you!" Alex shouted back.

"How could you say that to your own father?"

"Whatever, you don't care. You're just mad because there's no beer here!" There was a wildness to Alex's voice. Like a cry trying to escape.

"You're never going to let that go, are you?" his father asked gruffly, crossing his arms.

Alex threw up his arms. "*Let that go*? Like it was no big deal? All you did was drink and beat us."

"You don't know what it was like for me. I worked all day and I still couldn't afford all the bills. Credit card companies were calling me all the time," his father said. His shoulders slouched thinking about it.

"Oh, boo-hoo. Do you think I would actually feel bad for you? You're crazy. I still got bruises from you." Alex held up his arms, sliding back the sleeves.

His father frowned. "Do you remember why I gave you that whoopin'? Because you stole candy from the store. You know that's not right."

"Ooh, look who's all high and mighty? In case you forgot, you're in Hell, too!" Alex's voice rose higher. "Get the hell away from me!"

Alex stormed away. His father watched him go with a pained expression on his face. Then he slammed the door shut.

Dante stood there still. He was still processing what happened, trying to make sense of it. With a sigh, he went after Alex. He saw Alex had walked around the back of the shack. Following his trail, he found him under a few scraggly trees. He was kicking the dirt and muttering to himself.

"Hey," Dante said.

"We got to get out of here. I can't take this. I didn't shoot that bastard to be stuck with him here forever."

With a pang of sympathy, he remembered the first time he met Alex. He had said something about never having to deal with that crap again and how it was all over. Dante had said it only had begun. He didn't know how right he was.

Dante shook his head. "No, we can't."

"What do you mean? We can. We'll try again. We'll get it this time, I know we will," Alex said. His eyes were wild, and he flailed his arms while he talked.

Dante thought about his conversation with Eva. She had died from a drug overdose. She wasn't trying to kill herself. She was trying to escape—escape from her problems. Same with Alex's father. He made his life and Alex's life substantially worse by drinking to escape his problems. *And what about me? I'm no better. I thought I could escape my consequences. I thought I could escape from myself, from being a reaper. I thought I could escape from Hell. I was wrong. About all of it.*

"Alex, tell me why you jumped off the bridge."

Alex's face scrunched up. "Why do you want to know?"

"Just tell me."

Alex sighed and dropped his arms. He stared off in the distance, not meeting Dante's eyes. "I thought everything would be better once dad was gone. But it wasn't. It got worse. People came around, looking for the money my dad borrowed. And since he wasn't around, they came after me. I tried to get a job, but it didn't pay nearly enough. So then I started stealing money. The cops started sniffing around for me, and I knew it was only a matter of time before I got caught. And I didn't want to rot away in jail. So yeah, that's why I jumped. I figured being dead was better." He sighed again and closed his eyes. "I wanted it to be over."

"But that's just it," Dante said. "You can't escape from your problems. Neither can I. I can't escape being a reaper, and I can't escape from here."

"But that's bullshit! You know you can escape from here! You don't want to, so now I'm stuck here, too!"

"Alex, listen—"

"No, you listen. You failed one time, and now you want to give up?"

Dante hung his head. "What do you think is going to happen to us if we actually do get out of here? Do you really think we'll be able to just hang out? The angels will only send us back here."

"And what about the whole 'break into heaven' part?"

"I don't know what I was thinking. That would never happen." Dante's eyes fell to the ground.

"I can't believe you're giving up!" Alex pulled at his hair.

"Alex—"

"Leave me alone," Alex said as he walked away.

***

Dante laid on his side, listening to the snores. He tried to sleep, but the conversation with Alex kept repeating in his head.

He shouldn't keep trying to escape his problems, but Alex raised a good point. Was he giving up then? What did it mean to give up? His eyes wandered around the dingy shack. This is what it meant. Every day he would wake up and work in the fields in the hot sun to then return here to start all over again. The days stretched before him. *But even if we do escape—if Lucifer doesn't get us first—then the angels will. And we'll be right back where we started. It seems like we can't win at all.*

He wished he could see Sophia. He wondered where she was and if he could find her. A memory flashed in front of his eyes and his hands flew to his inner pocket. *It's still here!* The feather's edge was so soft and slightly tickled. In the dark, he could only see with his fingers. But it was Sophia's feather. After everything that happened, he completely forgot about it. Now, he clutched it. *This is all I have left of her.*

His conversation with Alex ran through his mind again. Was he giving up? What about his promise to Sophia? Was he giving up on that, too? Maybe Alex was right. Questions were piling up in his head again.

Dante rubbed his eyes, finally feeling tired. He wanted to talk to Alex but it would have to wait till later. Now was time for sleep.

***

Dante nudged Alex awake. The morning light peeked through the cracks in the door.

"Hey," Dante said softly.

"Hey yourself. Go back to sleep," Alex groaned, thrashing around.

"I need to talk to you."

"And I don't want to talk to you." Alex pulled the ragged blanket over his head.

Dante sighed at the blanket. "Look, I'm sorry."

"I don't give a shit." Alex's voice was muffled.

"You were right," Dante continued. "I was giving up. And I don't want to anymore. I want to try."

Alex was quiet for a moment, and then sat up. The blanket fell off of him. "You want to try to get out Hell, you mean?"

"Yes," Dante said firmly.

"What changed your mind?" Alex asked. He looked dubious.

"You did. I thought I was trying to escape my problems. But I'm not. I'm going to go right to the top and get all my questions answered. It's not an escape. It's my goal."

"Then what are you waiting for? Let's go!"

"But there's one thing we have to do before we go."

Alex rolled his eyes. "I know, we gotta go get your girlfriend."

"Sophia is not my girlfriend," Dante said, grinding his teeth.

Alex smiled wickedly. "How did you know I was talking about her?"

Dante sighed and shook his head, knowing he fell for it.

"No, that's not what I meant," Dante said. "Before we make another escape, you need to tell your father what you did."

Alex shot him a deadly look. "And why do I need to do that?" His voice ran cold.

"Because you need to tell the truth."

"Why do you care?"

Dante held his gaze. "Tell me that it doesn't make you feel guilty for what you did."

"Why do you care?" His voice strained as he repeated his question.

"Because I'm not having you escape from your problems. You need to face your father and tell him. Only then can you come with me." Dante held firm, keeping his gaze steady. Alex would probably hate him, but he knew it needed to be done. And this way, Dante knew Alex had a good heart and could finally forgive him for what happened with Ryan.

"I'm not doing that," Alex said, crossing his arms.

"Then, we're not getting out of here," Dante said and shrugged. He kept his voice calm and his face neutral. He expected a backlash. He hoped that with time, Alex would follow through with his request.

***

Days went by, but it was hard to keep track of the monotony.

Wheels creaked and groaned under the weight of grain. Dante followed the sinners pushing the wagon. The shadows were long and the air was chilly. Another day gone. Dante couldn't stand reaping anymore. He was ready to throw his scythe away.

They came upon the little shack, which seemed almost homely now, in some weird, twisted way. It was the only place where Dante was allowed to rest away from the wheat, away from the sun. And to let him sleep—a temporary escape.

One of the demons threw a moldy loaf of bread at him. Dante's supper. He sighed, wishing he never complained about reaper food. He caught Alex's eye. Alex was sitting in the shade of the shack, already eating his bread. He didn't even bat an eye at the colorful mold on the loaf. It was amazing how he easily adapted. He looked so nonchalant, like none of this was a big deal. Dante half-smiled, remembering why he was friends with Alex in the first place.

"What are you smiling at?" Alex asked with a scowl. He bit off another piece of bread.

Dante's smile grew. "You."

Alex gave him a hard look. "Are you making fun of me?"

"No, not at all," Dante said and sat next to him.

Alex side-eyed him. "Am I going to get another lecture about what I should be doing?"

"I should have never given you an ultimatum. I shouldn't force you to do something you don't want to do. It wasn't right for me to do that. I know we have all made mistakes—that's why we're here, right?"

Dante had a lot of time to think. And it didn't feel right to leave without Alex. It was partly because of Alex that Dante wanted to stop reaping in the first place. A lot had changed from when he first met him on the Golden Gate Bridge. Alex had been with him since the beginning. And Dante wanted Alex to be with him till the end.

Alex sighed. "I know I've been an ass. And I know I should tell him. But I can't." Alex met Dante's eyes. "Just so you know, I do feel guilty for what I did. It keeps me up at night. And when I do fall asleep, that's all I dream about. But to actually confess that to him.... Well, it makes me realize I'm no better than him. Maybe, I'm even worse."

Alex fell into silence. Dante lowered his eyes, not knowing what to say. A hot breeze blew by, kicking up the scattered ash. But that wasn't all. The wind brought something else with it—a smell Dante couldn't identify.

He breathed in deeply, trying to figure out what the smell was. "What is that?"

"What's what?" Alex asked, sniffing the air. "Wait, that smells like wine. But, where is it coming from?"

Dante felt the wind and turned to face it. "The wind is coming from that direction. Let's follow it." He was curious because he hadn't seen any alcohol the whole time he was here. The only time he even saw a hint of it was in the great dining hall, but that wine was old and dried up. This was potent and fresh.

"We should go check it out," Alex said with a grin.

They walked away from the shack and across scraggly ground covered in stubborn weeds. In the distance there was a cluster of scrawny pine trees. The tree branches waved in the wind.

"Hey, if nothing else, we could always get some more yummy bark," Alex said. His smile faded from his lips as he realized what he said. It was impossible to think about bark without conjuring up the images of Ryan's death.

Alex scowled. "Forget I ever said anything," he said quickly.

"Don't worry about it," Dante said. "I've thought a lot about it and I don't blame you for what happened. I don't think anyone could have saved him."

Dante still wasn't sure what he saw and the more he replayed the images in his head, the more distorted everything became until he didn't know what the truth was. But he did know that in the end, it didn't really matter. Nothing could bring Ryan back and pointing fingers wasn't going to help anyone. And it was nice to have his friend back.

They came upon the trees and stopped when they heard laughter. The unexpected sound made Dante's heart race. He almost laughed at himself for getting so scared.

Dante and Alex looked at each other in confusion. It wasn't common to hear people enjoying themselves. It *was* Hell, after all.

They ducked under the tree branches and found a small group of sinners. They were all sitting in a circle, passing a bottle around. One man took the bottle and a big swig. As he dropped his arm, Dante recognized him as Alex's father.

"Dad, what the hell?" Alex asked. His hands clenched into fists.

"Ah, my boy, guess what we found?" His father sloshed the bottle around. "Come join us!" He laughed boisterously.

The others laughed too, as if he said something funny. It was obvious they all had been drinking for a while. Dante glanced at the other faces. He was surprised to see Eva among them. Her cheeks were flushed and she giggled excessively.

"Eva!" Alex said, shocked.

She giggled again. "You can sit here." She patted the spot next to her.

Dante expected Alex to jump at the opportunity. But his face contorted into a grimace. Dante guessed it was the juxtaposition of seeing Eva and his father in the vicinity and both drunk.

"I can't believe this," Alex said sharply, cutting through the laughter.

"Alex, what's wrong?" Eva asked.

Alex never took his eyes off his father. "I should've known. Of course you would be drinking. What's your excuse now?"

"Oh, liven up. Look around you!" He threw out his arms. "We're in the worst possible place, getting worked to the bone every day. Why not try to have some fun." He took another swig from the bottle. "And keep our spirits up!" He added, laughing.

Alex rushed forward and knocked the bottle out his hands. It clattered on the ground, spilling out the rest of its contents.

"What's your problem?" his father asked, his voice raising. "Why did you do that?"

"Do you really have to ask? I can't stand to see you drunk for another minute! All those times—" His breath caught, unable to say anymore. A tortured look seized his face.

"Those times are done," his father said gruffly. "I'm paying the price for it, yeah?"

"No, not nearly enough punishment for you." Alex's voice was hoarse and hollow.

"Oh, yeah? And what about you? I'm not surprised to see you here, son," he sneered.

"Shut up, just shut up!" Alex shouted. His hands flew to his ears.

His father opened his mouth to say more, but Alex cut him off.

"I'm glad I shot you," Alex said. He let the silence hang on his words.

His father gaped at him. "What did you say?"

Alex lifted his chin. His eyes were set. "You heard me."

His father's hand grasped at his chest. "You killed me? My own son?" he asked slowly in disbelief. His eyes glazed over and he grew very still.

Alex stood there, staring at his father. They were both caught in time, so still like statues. Minutes went by. Everyone else was silent, watching them, waiting to see what would happen.

"You really do hate me, don't you?" his father asked. His voice was mournful.

"Yeah."

His father looked away, nodding. "I know I haven't been a good father to you. And I know saying sorry isn't enough. But it's all I can do," he continued, meeting Alex's eyes again. "I'm sorry."

Alex still hadn't moved this whole time. But now he did. He turned and walked away.

Dante went after him, not knowing what to say. He didn't expect that turn of events, and he wasn't sure what to make of it. He followed Alex back to the shack, and they got their allotted bread and water in silence. Dante kept trying to read Alex's expression on his face. But his face was neutral, unreadable. Dante wasn't sure what to say still, so he stayed by him for moral support.

By now, the sun had set, and the darkness had settled in for the night. The other sinners were starting to go to sleep, but Alex still hadn't said a word yet. Dante felt his own body beg for rest, his limbs heavy with sleep. As he began to slip away, he heard Alex speak.

"I never expected him to apologize. I honestly don't know what to do with that."

Thick with sleep, Dante replied, "Forgive him."

If Alex said anything else, Dante didn't hear it. He was already fast asleep.

Chapter 25

He felt a pressure on his shoulder. Rubbing the last of the sleep out of his eyes, he was face to face with Alex. Seeing him made all the memories from the night before come rushing back. Dante sat up. There was an intense look in his eyes and an urgency in the air.

"What's wrong?" Dante asked.

"They're gone."

Dante rubbed his eyes again as if that was going to help him understand. "What're you talking about?"

Alex nodded over his shoulder. "Everyone who was—how should I say?—*partaking in spirits* is gone. They never came back last night."

Dante was trying to process all this while wondering how Alex never seemed to sleep. "So what do you think that means?" he asked.

Alex's face soured. "Nothing good."

Dante's eyes flickered around the cramped space. There were a lot of empty beds. Crumpled blankets laid in the places where there were once bodies. The absences hung heavy in the air.

The door slammed open and a scaly demon stomped through. His yellow slitted eyes narrowed at them.

"Everyone get up," the demon demanded.

The few other sinners yawned and stretched awake.

The demon grimaced. "I said get up!" He said as he snapped his whip in the air.

Everyone, including Dante and Alex, scrambled to their feet.

"Now, I'm sure you have noticed there's less of you here," the demon continued. He paused and smiled while the sinners glanced around and murmured to themselves. "That's what happens when you steal wine from us and spend the night drinking. You all should know by now there's consequences for your actions. That's why you're here, right?" He laughed, but everyone else cold-stone stared at the demon.

Dante held his breath, waiting to hear the demon confirm his suspicions.

"We fed them to the hellhounds," the demon said. His pointy fangs gleamed. "They screamed the whole time."

Dante's eyes widened. It wasn't just Alex's father. It was Eva, too. *What a horrible way to go.*

The demon met everyone's eyes to make sure the message was clear. "So don't get any ideas." He cracked the whip again. "Now, get moving!"

Everyone shuffled out without a word.

The news stunned Dante. He never imagined it would be the last time he would see those people alive. Hanging his head, he knew he shouldn't have delayed. He could have gotten Eva out of here earlier. But now it was too late. He glanced over at Alex. No way was he going to make that mistake again.

Before they parted ways to go work, Dante nudged Alex. "We gotta escape," he whispered.

Alex nodded numbly, his face pale.

At the crack of the whip, they separated. Dante took up his scythe for another grueling day of reaping.

***

Dante went to share his moldy dinner with Alex when he realized Alex was nowhere to be seen. He hadn't seen him since this morning. He wondered if Alex was still reeling from what happened to his dad and Eva. Alex never looked so dejected. But where could he be? Alex had committed suicide once. What if he tried again? At the thought, he threw down the bread and scrambled out of the shack.

All around were endless wheat fields. He darted, scanning as he went. Desperately, he searched for any hint of Alex. But nothing. He stopped, catching his breath. *I need to think instead of blindly running in circles. That's not helping anyone.* His heart was hammering as hard as ever but he didn't let that distract him.

Where could he be? He let his thoughts rush around him. Memories floated to the surface but he let them drift by if they didn't help. One memory snagged and he focused on it. It was from the other night when the smell of wine was in the air—the last time Alex ever saw his dad and Eva. *Do I remember where that is? That's right, Alex made a joke about bark because we saw pine trees.*

That's it! Pumping his arms and legs, he raced toward the trees, hoping it wasn't too late. As he drew closer, the pine trees stretched higher in the sky. The thin, knotty branches looked so frail a strong breeze could knock them over.

There was Alex.

Dante had been searching for him for so long he almost didn't believe his eyes when he saw him. Like it was such a strong desire that he conjured him from his mind.

Alex didn't notice him which was surprising because Dante wasn't exactly being quiet with all his heavy breathing. But Alex seemed to be lost in thought. His back was to him and he was staring at something.

Dante slowly walked up to him, not wanting to disturb the moment.

Alex held his own scythe in his hand. It was only a normal scythe that was only good for harvesting wheat. But he used it to dig graves. Alex pushed the last of the dirt on the mounds and wiped his brow.

So that's what he had been doing. Dante's heart tugged at the sight.

Alex stood up and finally noticed him. "What are you doing here?"

Dante stared at the graves. "Paying respects."

"I almost wish we had flowers. It doesn't seem right without them." Alex's voice was quiet and forlorn with no hint of sarcasm at all. It didn't even sound like him.

Dante picked up a few fallen stalks of wheat and carefully laid them in the middle of the mounds, one by one. "Unfortunately, this will have to do," he said.

Alex nodded. He went to the last one and stopped in front of it. "This is where my dad is buried. I remember standing at his grave the first time. And here I am again. At least it wasn't my fault this time." He let out a short laugh but it sounded like a bark. Tears flooded his eyes. "I really am a horrible person."

Dante's heart went out to him. "Last time I told you to forgive him. Now I think you should forgive yourself."

Alex fell to his knees. "How can I?" He wept, tears streaming down his face.

Dante knelt down and began to pray. God seemed to listen last time. Maybe He would now, too.

He didn't know how long they stayed there. Time slowed and stretched until he lost track. Only when the shadows blanketed the ground did he know it was getting late. He prodded Alex to go and silently they left together.

***

By the time they got back, it was dark and the bread was all gone. Moldy and gross as it was, it was still edible and the others had already helped themselves to it. *Just as well.* Dante laid back with his stomach growling. *It was worth it to find Alex.*

Thinking of him, Dante glanced over. Alex was still quiet but the ghostly look was gone. His eyes reflected the flames of the candle as he stared at it.

The silence followed them here. Empty spots on the floor were the reminders of those who once slept there.

"We need to escape now. I can't take this anymore." Alex finally spoke.

"Even if we do escape again," Dante said. "We'll have to get by Cerberus. I doubt he'll let us cross again."

"Not this time," Alex said. "We're not in the city anymore, remember? Out here in the fields, we can use the wheat as cover as we run away."

Dante thought for a second. "You do realize the demons can fly, right? They can see us from above."

"Not if they're distracted." Alex was determined not to give up. Dante wondered how he could keep going like this. He noticed Alex hadn't said anything more about his father or Eva. He didn't know how to broach the subject. They both were determined to get out of here this time and now they had no reason to linger anymore.

"This isn't your first time doing something like this, is it?" Dante's question sounded accusatory, but he smiled as he said it.

Alex grinned wickedly.

Laughter bubbled in Dante. For a moment, he was transported back in time when he first met Alex. Alex was his first comrade in arms, his first conspirator, his friend. Any mistrust he had before had melted away as they chuckled together.

Maybe this is for nothing. But I have to try. What else is there to lose besides hope? Hope is the only thing I can cling to. Maybe hope is worthless. But not having hope? Somehow, that is even less.

He leaned against the rough wooden wall. Cold night air blew between the gaps in the boards. He shivered. Soon morning would come. He knew if they were really going to try to escape, then they needed to do it tomorrow.

***

Sometime in the night, Dante must have fallen asleep because the next thing he knew, the door banged open.

"Get up!" The harsh voice of a demon yelled.

Moaning and grumbling, they all rose. Alex stretched his arms, sending Dante a wink around the crook of his arm.

Well, it looks like Alex hasn't lost his nerve. Neither will I. A knot of determination tightened in his chest.

They stumbled out into the fresh air. After being cooped up in the shack, he had gotten used to the stale air. The sun hadn't had a chance to scorch the sky and land yet, but by the intense rays, he knew it would be heating up soon. Every day was hot, and the sun was relentless. *I guess it doesn't rain often.* He hadn't even seen rain since he came here.

The whip cracked like thunder. "Get to work!" the demons hissed.

His back burned in protest as he swung his scythe. The wheat swayed before him while the stalks behind him laid dead in his wake.

He kept glancing around, waiting to see when he could make his escape. But it seemed like the demons knew something was amiss. There was always a demon making rounds while another flew in the sky, circling them like vultures. Maybe he was blind to it before, but it was impossible to find a way to slip out.

Remembering Alex's words, Dante wondered about making a distraction. They never did get to elaborate on that plan—if there was even a plan in the first place.

The air quickly grew hot. *If I'm going to do something, I need to do it soon.* He already felt the energy leaving his body.

Between swings, he racked his brain for an idea of a distraction. What he really wanted was a way to obscure the demons' vision so they could slip away unnoticed.

The wheat fell, rustling like straw because it was so dry. The ends of wheat scattered like dust on the parched ground.

It hasn't rained in a long time.

It would only take a spark to ignite the whole thing. Dante was surprised the hot ash from the city didn't set the fields aflame already.

And he knew how to start a fire from Ryan. Dante sent a silent prayer to wherever Ryan's soul was now. Hopefully, it was better than this.

He waited until the demon's back was turned and then he slipped out the flint and steel from his inner pocket. He only had a moment to do this. If he messed up, he might not get another chance.

He struck the pieces next to the pile of fallen wheat. But his aching hands didn't want to cooperate. He couldn't get a spark.

"Hey, you! Get up and get back to work!"

Too late. He was already found out. But his trembling fingers were on autopilot. He struck the flint again and a spark flared to life.

The demon pulled him to his feet.

"What do you think you're doing?" the demon spat.

Dante hid the flint in his fist, hoping the demon didn't see.

"I'm tired," Dante said.

"You need some motivation." The demon raised his whip.

Dante braced for the impact, but it never came.

"Fire!" the demon yelled.

Dante followed the demon's gaze. It wasn't a spark anymore. It was a wildfire. And it grew before his eyes as it engulfed the dry wheat.

Now was the time. He yanked out of the demon's grip and ran. He didn't know where he was running. But he dove into the wheat field for cover—the part that wasn't on fire yet.

The smoke filled the air above him. The wheat slapped his face as he raced by. Until suddenly, it didn't. He stopped as he realized he was in an open field laid bare of stalks.

He tensed, frightened.

"What are you doing?" Alex asked. He was covered in sweat with a scythe in his hands.

"Getting out of here."

Alex smirked. "I knew you could do it."

They didn't waste any more time. They ran in stride. Dante hooked his scythe on his back, allowing him to pump his arms better. Alex had no such luck. He could only carry his scythe in his hand, out in front of him.

"Where are we going?" Dante asked, huffing already. He was annoyed his energy was leaving his body so quickly. They had barely crossed the open field.

Alex sucked in his breath. It seemed he was also feeling the effects of their sprint.

"Don't know, don't care," he replied.

"We have to get Sophia."

"Of course." Alex rolled his eyes. "How are we even going to find her?"

Dante gasped for breath as they continued to run. In the distance, he could see another wheat field to hide in.

"We're going to have to go into the center of the city," Dante said. He wasn't sure if Sophia would be there, but it would be a place to start.

"Oh, come on," Alex said. "So we're going to have to backtrack *and* go right where Lucifer is? Are you trying to get us killed? How do you even know you can find her?"

"I didn't think this all the way through. But I made her a promise."

Alex scowled, but he relented with a "Fine."

They kept running until they reached the safety of the wheat field. Among the stalks of wheat, the air was humid and musty, making it hard to breathe.

A shriek cried from above. Dante's blood ran cold. They dove to the ground, hiding in the field as best as they could. Over the sounds of their heavy breathing, Dante heard screams in the distance. It seemed like the distraction was still working. There was still hope.

"Okay, so which way?" Alex asked.

Dante looked around, but they were surrounded by stalks. He peeked over the wheat. To his right, he saw the walls of the city. He checked the position of the sun. If he kept the sun to his left, then he knew he would be heading in the right direction while crouching in the safety of the wheat.

"Follow me," Dante said and they both kept their heads bowed as they weaved through the field.

Dante kept glancing at the sun to confirm they were headed in the right direction. But he was also checking for anything else in the sky. Between the demons, Furies, and Lucifer, there were too many evil things that could fly.

They kept going like that for a while. Dante couldn't tell how much time had passed, but it was enough for his back to ache from being bent over. He kept listening and watching the skies, but they were in the clear. It was almost too easy. Somehow, that made Dante even more nervous, like he must have forgotten something.

The wheat field ended abruptly and they found themselves on a river bank. The water cut right through the wheat fields and snaked to the city. Unfortunately, the space between the wheat field and the city was barren of anything to hide under, in, or around. Only pitiful grass poked out of the ground, no good to anyone.

"Shit," Alex said.

Dante sighed. The good luck couldn't last.

A growl came behind Dante. His hair on the back of his neck stood up. Instinctively, he reached for his scythe and spun around with his weapon at the ready.

Flaming red eyes stared back at him. Its growls grew from deep in its throat, and its fangs were slick with blood. A hellhound.

Of course. How could I forget about hellhounds? Despair pooled in his veins.

"Dante, watch out!" Alex yelled.

The hellhound lunged at him, jaws open. Dante fell back. Hot breath and fangs followed, pushing him into the ground. The weight of the dog was too much. He couldn't get back up. The dog snarled, fangs dangerously close to his face. He struggled to shove the hellhound away. His hands sunk into its mangy fur until he felt the strained sinews of its neck as it tried to bite him.

Dante gasped in the hot, stinky breath while he gathered the last remaining strength he had. He quickly shifted his weight over to the side. Faltering, the dog was unbalanced and toppled off of him.

He scurried to his feet and gulped in a few deep breaths. He was winded and his arms were already weary. And he didn't even hurt the hellhound. Not even one scratch.

Alex took this opportunity to attack. He swung his scythe at the hellhound. The dog snapped the weapon in two with its powerful jaws. Alex gasped in horror as the weapon fell useless to the ground.

Dante stared at the broken scythe. He glanced back at his own scythe in his hands. It didn't take much to realize weapons weren't much use. This hellhound seemed even more powerful than the ones they encountered before. Maybe that was why it was by itself and not in a pack like the others.

The hellhound whipped around and faced Dante again, snarling.

Dante froze as he tried to think of a way out of this.

"Hey, doggie," he said in his nicest, please-don't-kill-me voice.

Alex threw his hands up. "What're you doing?" he asked, bewildered. "That could be the same hellhound that killed my dad, Eva, and all the others."

"I'm trying to make sure it doesn't kill us, too," Dante said, keeping his eyes locked on the hellhound.

The dog barked in reply. Dante had just enough time to think his foolish idea worked before the fangs were out again. The hellhound lunged at him. He was quicker this time and side-stepped it. But he couldn't keep dodging it forever.

He backed away from the dog, trying to keep his distance so he would have more time to react. As he stepped back, he tripped over a pile of bones—human bones. The dog growled as it drew nearer.

Dante cursed. He was truly screwed. A sickening feeling overcame him. *My bones will soon join theirs.* He launched a bone out of anger and frustration.

The hellhound barked and ran after it. Laying on the ground, it clamped the bone between its huge paws and slobbered all over it. Then it growled at Dante like he was trying to take the bone away.

"I don't want the bone, okay? It's all yours," Dante said, keeping his voice higher.

The hellhound growled again, but it was much more distracted now, munching happily. He had never been around a hellhound like this before. It seemed so normal, not scary or threatening. The hellhound was looking at him like he was interrupting its private time. *Maybe that's why it was so mad at me. Maybe I wandered into its territory, so it thought I was an intruder.*

He picked up another bone, a femur yellowed with age. The dog eyed it with its flaming red irises, waiting to see what he would do. Dante waggled the bone in front of him. The dog's ears perked up, and it wagged its tail. Now he had its attention, he threw the bone. The dog scampered off after it, snatching it in its jaws. Instantly, the dog crunched the bone as if it was nothing more than an apple.

Dante's stomach flip-flopped as he thought about how its jaws were only inches away from his face. *That could've been me.*

"Good doggie," he said in his high-pitched voice.

Alex rolled his eyes but didn't say anything.

The hellhound barked in reply.

"We should go now," Dante said in falsetto. He was eager to get away. He didn't know how long this could go on and he was running out of bones that weren't attached to him.

He moved deliberately, making sure to not scare or upset the hellhound who was still munching away. He motioned Alex to follow him. They both carefully stepped away. Dante held his breath and turned to go.

He was only a few footsteps in when he heard shuffling behind him. It was the dog. Dante was covered in cold sweat. There was no way they could get away now.

Dante turned to face the hellhound. It sat back on its haunches. Its eyes were big and mournful. In its mouth, it held another bone that stuck out at either end of its jaw. A hand was still attached, hanging by a thread of skin. When the dog cocked his head, the hand swung. It seemed like it was trying to communicate.

"You want me to throw the bone?" Dante asked in disbelief.

The dog got up, tail wagging.

Unsure, he walked closer with his hand outstretched. It let him take the bone. It was warm and slick with slobber. The bony hand swung wildly and then plopped on the ground. The dog eagerly snatched it up and gobbled it up. Then it looked at Dante to throw the bone.

Oh, sure, why not? I'm only on the run with a horde of demons after me trying to rescue a fallen angel from Lucifer's clutches before escaping Hell. But yeah, why not play fetch right now? Dante couldn't believe the predicament he was in. But if he didn't play along, the hellhound would be chomping on his corpse.

He threw the bone—harder this time, really letting it fly. With an excited bark, the hellhound tore off after it. A moment later, the dog came back with its prized bone and placed it at his feet.

Dante looked exasperatedly at Alex. They needed to get moving. Was he going to be stuck here, endlessly playing fetch until one of the demons caught them?

Alex frowned, thinking. "What if we keep playing fetch in the direction we want to go?"

Dante nodded and tossed the bone in the direction of the city. As the hellhound clambered to it, they walked closer. When the dog retrieved the bone, Dante threw it again in the same direction. And so, little by little, they reached the city.

Chapter 26

Smoke billowed from the ground and ash fluttered in the wind. Inside the city, it was smoldering rubble. Dante expected the city to be more in the process of being rebuilt after Lucifer's villainous speeches. But it looked the same except that the lava had subsided and cooled and hardened to black.

They picked their way through the debris and ash. Some spots were still hot with coals, which were hidden until their feet found them. The hellhound was lucky since heat didn't affect it. It only sniffed at the flames with disinterest.

Dante glanced at the dog. It finally stopped wanting to play fetch by the time they got to the city. He guessed exploring the ruins was more exciting.

The hellhound stopped and pawed at the ground. It whined and poked its snout in the ash. And when it emerged, it had another bone in its jaws as a prize. This time it was a piece of breastbone.

The dog continued to trot around with the ribs curving up from its jaws to around its head with the ends of the ribs sticking in its ear. Dante wanted to laugh at the ridiculousness of it all.

"We should name it," Alex said with a half-smile. "It's only right."

"It's our pet now?" Dante asked, shaking his head in disbelief. Only an hour or so ago, it was trying to bite his face off.

"I mean, what do you name a hellhound?" Alex mused, not answering the question.

Dante smiled. Even after everything that had happened to them, Alex was back to his normal self.

"What about Fluffy?" Dante offered.

Alex rolled his eyes. "That's horrible, no."

They laughed. It felt like such a relief.

"You know," Alex wondered out loud. "I thought Hell was all fire and brimstone. There isn't any fire—not really. But hellhounds are made of fire." He paused and looked into the hellhound's flaming red eyes.

"Brimstone," Alex announced with certainty. "That's his name."

"That's not a name. What about Brim? For short?"

Alex shrugged. "Sure, why not?"

Why not indeed. Dante learned to go with the flow in this weird place. He didn't know what to make of it. It wasn't anything like he expected.

But now he needed to focus on why they came here in the first place. *Sophia, where are you?* Everywhere he looked, there was smoke and ruins. How was he going to find her? Nothing was familiar. No clues to go on.

Without realizing it, Dante was following Brim. The hellhound went in front of them, sniffing through the wreckage—searching for bones, no doubt.

The ruined city was quiet as a graveyard. And going by the piles of bones everywhere, it wasn't far from the truth.

"To Brim, this must look like heaven," Alex mused as he eyed all the remains.

Dante grimaced but he had to agree. Brim happily trotted from one pile of bones to the next, dropping one bone to only pick up another one like he couldn't decide which he preferred.

He acts like a normal dog. As he watched Brim, an idea began to form. It seemed far-fetched and crazy, but so was everything else. He had to try.

Dante pulled out a feather. For some reason, he decided to keep Sophia's feather. Now it might prove useful. Brim was starting to get really far ahead of them, so Dante had to half-jog to catch up with it.

"Hey, doggie. Hey, Brim," he called. His voice slid higher.

The dog glanced in his direction, but it was already on a mission to pick out another prize in the ashes.

"Here." Dante waved the feather at the hellhound. "Come smell this."

Brim looked up from its newest treasure trove. It sniffed the air curiously and trotted to Dante.

He stretched out his arm. Brim breathed in, making the feather flutter and tinkle its nose. The dog sneezed.

"Can you follow the scent?" Dante asked.

"It's a hellhound, not a bloodhound," Alex said. "Do you really think this will work?"

"It's worth a try."

Brim started spinning in circles, sniffing and sneezing. Dante sighed. *So much for that.*

But then, the hellhound's ears perked up, and it bounded off, barking.

"Did that actually work?" Alex asked incredulously.

"He found something," Dante said and they ran off after it.

***

It was hard to keep up with Brim. It seemed to have found renewed energy as it leaped over debris.

Dante couldn't help but to be reminded of the first time he ran through the city. He never thought he would be running into the city. Of course, he never thought he would be trying to help an angel, either. He made a promise to her. But really, it was more than that. He didn't want to admit it, not even to himself.

Just when he wondered how much longer he could keep running, Brim stopped. Alex caught up to it first, then Dante came puffing behind. Dante couldn't tell what made Brim stop. But as he slowed to where the dog and Alex were, a cold dread filled him.

Lucifer.

Dante's knees were weak. He couldn't believe it. They escaped the demons and avoided getting eaten by a hellhound to only run straight into the devil himself.

The air was heavy with silence as they stared at each other. It seemed Lucifer was as surprised to see them as they were to see him.

Alex broke the spell first. He turned to Brim and said, "Bad doggie!"

Brim whined and ran off.

Alex cursed.

Maybe we shouldn't have trusted a hellhound.

Lucifer laughed. A long, belly-aching laugh. A mocking laugh. It grated Dante to the bone.

"You do realize you went the wrong way, right?" Lucifer asked, chuckling.

Dante's face was set in stone.

"When I heard you both escaped, I had my demons search the fields and mountains. I never dreamed you would run straight to me." Lucifer laughed again. "You are more foolish than I took you for."

Dante's heart knocked against his ribs. They messed up. He didn't know how or even if they could get out of this. He had blown the only chance they had to escape.

"So how are you going to learn your lesson this time? Harvesting the wheat wasn't enough of a punishment for you. What about—"

"Where is Sophia?" Dante interrupted. He had to know if Brim really led them astray or if the dog actually was trying to help them.

"Sophia? My daughter is right where she should be," Lucifer said. "Keep away from her, *reaper*." He grimaced as he said the word. "Besides, you shouldn't worry about her. You should be worrying about yourself. I'm not going to be merciful this time."

Where have I heard that before? This whole time he had been running in circles. Nothing has changed since he was in front of The

Council for the first time. Here he was, back in the city and helpless before Lucifer. Again. *How do I break this cycle?*

A barking sound broke his thoughts.

Brim bounded toward them with his tongue flopping. Seeing a hellhound running toward Dante gave him the chills. He wasn't sure if he would ever be comfortable with that.

But it wasn't just Brim. Following close behind him was Sophia. She looked better than he last saw her. She wore a clean, white robe and her hair was so golden, it gleamed. Her eyes were heavy with sadness, but when she saw Dante and Alex, her expression brightened.

"I couldn't understand why it wanted me to follow him," she said as Brim trotted up to Dante and licked him.

"Good dog," Dante said, patting his head.

Sophia looked at Dante in amazement. "How did you befriend a hellhound?"

Dante shrugged.

"His name's Brim," Alex said. "Short for Brimstone."

Sophia nodded. "Of course," she said sarcastically.

For a moment, it was like the last few weeks never happened. The three of them laughed. Nothing was really that funny. It was more like relief and joy at being reunited. Going through hell with someone was a bond that lasted a lifetime.

Brim barked, apparently wanting to be in on it.

Alex patted its head. "Sorry about before, buddy."

"Sophia," Lucifer thundered. "Get away from the sinner and reaper. You are not to mingle with the likes of them."

Sophia wavered at the sound of her father's voice.

"If you don't get away from them right now, I'll kill them both," Lucifer threatened.

Her eyes welled with tears as she looked mournfully at them.

"Sophia," Dante said. "We will get out of here, I promise. And you'll keep your promise to your mother." He held her gaze to reassure her what he said was true.

Sophia gave him a smile. Light shone in her eyes. "Why is it that you give me hope when I had none?" She repeated what she had said before, but it seemed like she meant it more now. Turning back to her father, she said, "You can't tell me what to do anymore."

"I can and I will," Lucifer said. Fire flashed in his eyes, and the air around him crackled with energy.

"What else are you going to do to me? You already clipped my wings. Kept me trapped here. Not anymore." Sophia turned to Dante and Alex. Her eyes were set. "This time we escape or die trying."

"There's the motivational speech I was looking for," Alex said with a smirk.

"You are to be my successor, Sophia. Don't you forget that. This all will be yours," Lucifer said, gazing around him.

Sophia grimaced. "I didn't think it could get any worse, but I was wrong. You destroyed a decaying city. There's nothing here to salvage."

Lucifer's eyes narrowed. "You disobey me, you insult me. Don't test me, daughter."

Lifting her chin, Sophia said, "I will not cower anymore. I refuse to be here for another moment."

"If you won't listen, then I won't spare you. Don't think because you are my daughter I won't kill you, too." Lucifer's voice was daggers. "You have disobeyed me for the last time."

Fear rose in Sophia's eyes, but she shook it away. "Death would be preferable to this prison."

"So be it," Lucifer said, straightening up. "You are all doomed to die." There was weight to his words like he had uttered an incantation. The very air shimmered and crackled.

A shriek screeched overhead. The sky was darkening—not from clouds, but from demons. Swarms of them.

Dante's heart stopped. He was shaking. All the brave talk was one thing. But they were in the center of the city with all of hell's angels swooping down on them.

Alex grabbed his arm. "Run!" he yelled.

Without another word, Sophia, Alex, and Dante all ran. Brim, too—although the hellhound didn't seem to understand the severity of the situation. He barked happily as he bounded along like this was a game.

Lucifer shouted, "Get them! There should be nothing left to them by the time you're done with them!"

At those words, Dante pumped his legs faster. The screeching grew louder. The demons were getting so close that he could hear the bat-like wings flapping.

"Can we get out of the city?" Dante asked breathlessly.

"Follow me," Sophia shouted over the shrieks. Her wings spanned out, flapping hard. She couldn't fly but that didn't mean she wasn't going to try. And it kept the weight off her ankle.

They leaped over debris and kicked up ash as they ran by. The rubble was a blur. Dante blindly followed Sophia. Doubt clung to him. He couldn't shake the feeling they were running to their deaths. *Even if we manage to get out of the city, there's no way we can outrun demons who can fly. It's just not possible. But then, where is Sophia taking us?*

Something glittery came into view as they sped past more wreckage. It was a river—the same one where Dante drank from so long ago.

"Follow the river," Sophia said, pointing.

The river snaked out of sight. He sighed. *I'm already exhausted. How can I possibly keep this up?* All his old wounds were opening back up, even despite wrapping them in cloth rags. Blood dripped from his eye and his shoulder while his back ached from the whippings.

The impossibility of everything was catching up with Dante, even more than the demons at his heels. It wasn't giving up hope—it was facing reality. *It's not going to happen. Not only won't we escape Hell, we'll die before we leave the city.*

He looked at Sophia and Alex beside him. *This might be the last time I see them.* He wanted to say some final words. Something meaningful. But he couldn't think of anything. And time was running out.

The river ran alongside them. The water rushed and swelled. They all sprinted with all their might, breathing hard.

The demons were close. So close. Claws tore Dante's robe, grasping him.

"Is this the end?" he asked, not expecting an answer. Desperation hung in the air.

Sophia's hair tousled in the wind as she looked around. "Jump in!" she cried.

"How's that going to help?" Alex asked.

"Just do it!" she said and without another word, she jumped into the river. The current was strong and it dragged her downstream—faster than they were running.

That was the answer Dante needed. He jumped in with Alex close behind him. His feet were swept from beneath him as he was also pulled into the water.

He glanced back to see Brim on the riverbank, barking frantically at him. Brim wasn't following them. Was this some animal instinct he didn't have?

He didn't have time to mull it over. He spun and dunked under as he tried to keep afloat. The churning currents roared in his ears. The sky was a blur above him. He couldn't look long enough to see how close the demons were. He could barely keep track of where Sophia and Alex were.

And then he fell.

The water plunged around him, succumbing to gravity, pulling him down with it. For a second, he was suspended in midair as water droplets separated out like rain, no longer a river—it was a waterfall.

Floating no longer, gravity yanked him down. He hurled faster and faster to the bottom far below. The air was as cold as his realization. He was going to die. His screams filled his lungs, his ears, his head. His whole body protested the inevitable. The sharp rocks at the bottom protruded like jaws, waiting to snatch their prey.

And so he fell.

Chapter 27

Whack. Whack. Whack. The sound and the pain became one. At first, Dante couldn't understand it. But as he opened his eyes, he saw the source of the sound.

A cane hovered above him, poised to hit him again. Dante snatched it before it could make contact.

"Oh, you're finally awake," said the voice attached to the cane.

Dante squinted, trying to see in the faint light. The voice sounded like it was a feeble old man, but the grip on the other end of the cane was strong.

"Why are you hitting me?" Dante grumbled.

"I want my money," the old man retorted.

"What are you talking about?" Dante asked. His head was still spinning. Images flashed through his mind. He had been falling to his death, about to hit rocks. He felt his robe. It was dry. His hands clenched at the cloth as his heart sped up. *What was going on?*

"Oh, you're not going to pay? Then I'm not bringing you across. I don't work for free, you know."

"No, I don't know," Dante said, getting more irritated.

He looked around, trying to regain his senses. He was sitting on a riverbank, but unlike the river he was in before, this river was underground. The ceiling of the cave was high above them, burying itself in the shadows. Long, thin stalactites stretched down as the sound of dripping water surrounded them. The river was still like black glass. One rowboat sat on the edge of the river with the only source of light—a lantern with a flickering candle in it.

"Reaper, I don't meet a lot of your kind, but you're not exempt. Cough it up."

"Okay, but I don't have any," Dante said. "Why do you need money anyway? What are you spending it on?"

Dante's eyes adjusted to the darkness and now he could see the man's face. Currently, it was scrunched up in annoyance—Dante was getting used to seeing that expression on people. His hair was wiry and stringy from the lack of care. Wrinkles on his face were so pronounced it looked like weathered bark on a tree.

"It's the toll to cross the river," the man said, pointing.

"Why do I want to cross it? What's on the other side?"

"You ask a lot of questions."

"And you don't answer any of them." Dante frowned and looked up at the ceiling of the cave. "Did I fall from up there?"

The old man laughed. "Fall? For a reaper, you don't have a lot of experience with death, do you?"

Dante's frown deepened.

But this time, the old man answered. "You didn't fall. You died."

Dante's eyes snapped back to the old man. "What do you mean?" His heart thumped harder in his chest.

"Oh, come on, don't you give me a hard time now. You heard me. You're dead."

"But I'm already in Hell. How can I die?"

The old man laughed again—a laugh like a parent gives when a child asks a silly question. "You think there's an end to all this? It never ends."

Dante shook his head. "What does that mean?"

"So are you going to pay me?"

Dante sighed, realizing he wasn't going to get anyway with this old man. He wondered what happened to Sophia and Alex. If he died, then they must have, too. They were both in the water with him.

"Have you seen a fallen angel or a sinner or even a hellhound?" Dante asked. He included Brim in the off-chance it did end up jumping in.

"No, I haven't." The old man cocked his head and squinted at him. "You keep odd company."

Dante's stomach sank at his words. Maybe he was the only one dead. Then he would never see them again. Then the bigger realization hit him. How was he ever going to escape Hell now? It all seemed impossible.

"Ah so," the old man stretched, making his joints pop and creak. "I guess you're going to be stuck here. Have fun."

And with that, he hobbled with his cane to the rowboat. Pushing it off the bank, he climbed in. When the old man dipped his cane in the water, Dante realized his cane wasn't a cane at all. It was an oar. And he used that oar to swiftly row away, taking the only light source with him.

The darkness quickly engulfed him. It felt like it was pressing in on him. The water dripping sounded like echoes of screams—it was so loud against the silence of the cave.

But as he stood there, he began to hear other noises. Groaning, shuffling. Dante's shoulders tensed as he focused on the sounds. His hand reached for the scythe that wasn't there. He silently cursed, feeling naked without it. There was no way for him to defend himself.

A voice groaned, louder this time. Hair stood up on the back of his neck. He didn't have a weapon, so he raised his fists instead. After all he had been through, he wasn't going down without a fight. As the shuffling continued, he tried to place where the sounds were coming from. The noises reverberated in the cave, but he guessed as best as he could and quietly moved toward it to gain the element of surprise.

Another moan came right in front of him. Electricity burned in his veins as he punched whatever it was. His fist made contact with skin and bone. Pain throbbed in his fingers.

The thing he punched made an even bigger noise like it fell to the ground.

Dante held his breath to not give away his location and raised his fists again, ready to strike.

"What the hell!" said a very familiar voice. "Who punched me?"

"Alex?" Dante asked in surprise.

"Dante, did you seriously hit me?"

"Well, in my defense, I normally don't find friendly things in Hell, so..."

Dante tried to squint in the dark to see Alex, but he couldn't even make out a shadowy outline.

"Are you okay?" Dante asked, dropping his arms.

Alex groaned again. "I guess."

"Alex? Dante?" another voice cried out.

"Sophia?" Dante called into the darkness. "Is that you?"

"Yes!"

Dante sighed in relief. They were all okay. Except they were dead. But that was just a minor inconvenience.

"Where are you? I can't see," Sophia said.

"Hold on," Dante replied.

He gripped his robe, ready to tear even more off when realization struck him. The hem was back—the robe wasn't torn anymore. *Odd.* He didn't give it any more thought as he ripped a strip of fabric. Rummaging around in the dark, he saw with his hands. He glided his fingers across the ground. Mostly it was stones and packed sand, cool and slightly damp. But then he felt a stick. The bark had fallen off, leaving only the smooth surface left. He grabbed it and wound the strip of cloth around it.

Feeling in his pocket, he pulled out the flint and steel. Hopefully, it will be useful once more. It took a few tries, but soon he made a make-shift torch. It wasn't very bright—it was barely more than a spark that threatened to smolder out if he breathed too hard.

"Can you see this?" Dante called out. He couldn't remember where her voice came from so he held it up higher.

"Yes! Stay there!"

As Sophia approached, her face glowed in the warm light. Her golden eyes sparkled. Dante smiled, glad that she was okay.

"Are we underground?" Alex asked, rubbing his jaw.

"It looks like a cave. Apparently, we died," Dante said.

"I'm dead, again? My luck keeps getting worse."

Sophia looked around. "What is this place? There's something strange going on here."

"Oh, it's only gotten strange now," Alex muttered. "Not before with the demons and the hellhounds and Lucifer himself. No, being stuck in a cave all by ourselves. Now that's strange."

As Alex talked, Dante tensed. "We're not the only ones here," he said in a hush.

Alex side-eyed him. "What do you mean?"

They fell into silence. Stones scattered. *Something was out there.* Dante squinted, trying to see outside the faint circle of light that surrounded them. More shuffling. He held out the torch in front of them. The flame was shaking. No, his whole arm was shaking. He held his breath.

A bone-white hand gripped his arm. The skin was thin and stretched. And its touch was ice cold. His heart shot through his mouth.

"It's not my fault," it said. The voice sounded as hollow as the cave they were in. The torch's light flickered on its face. Empty eyes stared at him. "Not my fault."

"I-I'm sorry," he stuttered. He gulped and tried to pull away but the hand only grasped him tighter.

"Not my fault!" Its mouth opened wide, screaming in his face. It was so close Dante had a crazy thought of it swallowing him whole.

"Get lost!" Alex pushed it away, breaking its grip on Dante.

It hissed at him and sulked back into the shadows.

"What was that thing?" Dante asked. He shuddered at the image of it still etched in his mind.

"I don't know but I would call it a zombie," Alex replied.

It returned with more of its kind. The light seemed to attract them. They swarmed to them, pulling at them, muttering with wild looks in their eyes.

Dante, Alex, and Sophia huddled together.

"I think they're the sinners who died in Hell, but they aren't even human anymore," Sophia said, horrified. "Is this what will become of us?"

Before Dante could answer, another light bobbed in the distance. The wooden boat creaked as it banked the shore once more. Ripples in the water shimmered in the light. And with the thud of the oar, the old man climbed out of the boat.

Sophia and Alex ran to him. "Let us cross! We don't want to be here anymore! Please!" They were both begging at the same time that Dante wasn't sure who said what. Only Dante hung back, knowing what the old man was going to say.

"You need to pay the toll to cross the river."

"Toll?" Sophia and Alex said together.

"Old man, I told you, we don't have any money," Dante said.

"Speak for yourself," Sophia said and promptly pulled out a coin purse. "How much is it?"

"Three coins, one for each of you."

Sophia dropped the fee into the old man's hands.

The old man's face twisted into a smile as he pocketed the money.

"I guess you're rich if you're Lucifer's daughter," Alex muttered.

Sophia pretended not to hear him, but her lips curved down at the corners.

The old man pointed to the rowboat. "Get in," he said.

They all obliged, even Dante. He sighed in relief, letting his breath blow out his torch. *I don't need this right now.* He still held on to it, not knowing what to expect.

The boat wasn't very big, so they had to squish together with the old man at the other end, oars in hand. The water sloshed and the boat rocked each time the old man paddled. The lantern bobbed along, the flame flickering frantically. Dante peered into the darkness but it was so thick that even the light couldn't pierce it. The air was chilly as if the water below them was sucking out any warmth it could find.

"So where are we?" Dante asked. *If I died, then am I still in Hell?*

"Styx," the old man replied.

Dante waited for the reply to make sense. When it didn't, he responded, "Sticks?"

"No, Styx."

"I literally said the same thing you did," Dante said, feeling the irritation rise in his voice.

"This is the river Styx."

"That's a stupid name for a river," Alex said.

"No one asked you," the old man said gruffly.

"And what is your name?" Sophia asked.

"Charon."

Sophia shook her head. A puzzled look crossed her face. "Why is it that I have spent my whole life in Hell, but I have never heard of you or of this place?"

"That's because you're not in Hell," Charon said.

"I'm not?"

"We're in Hades," Charon said as if that explained everything.

They all were silent, trying to make sense of it.

"So like the whole Zeus and thunderbolt thing is real? Are we going to see him, too?" Alex cocked his head.

"Don't be ridiculous. Zeus is not in Hades."

"Riiight, I'm the one being ridiculous," Alex said. Dante couldn't see him roll his eyes, but he could sense it anyway.

"But this isn't Hell," Sophia said slowly. "How can that be?"

"Where do you think you go when you die?"

"Another level of Hell." Sophia shrugged.

Charon pursed his lips. "You're not wrong." He pulled up the oars. "We're here."

The boat slammed against the shore, and everyone lurched forward. They all climbed out of the boat. Stones crunched under Dante's feet, and water lapped around his ankles. It was so cold it instantly chilled his bones. Shivering, he hurried up the bank to get out of the water.

"And what's so special over here that we had to pay?" Alex asked.

The darkness was still so pervasive that Dante lit his torch again. The light radiated out and illuminated a bigger space around them. At first, there didn't seem much to see. It was a huge cave with stalagmites and stalactites aplenty, looking like pillars connecting the top and bottom. But then Dante noticed a hand laying on the ground. Then a pair of feet. Then a few legs. As his eyes adjusted, the darkness lifted. And all around them were bodies sprawled out, hundreds of them.

"Are they dead?" Dante asked, shocked.

"Close," Charon said. "They're sleeping."

Chapter 28

"Sleeping? All of them?" Dante couldn't believe it. It looked as though they had dropped right where they stood. He knelt down to a woman who lay close by. Inspecting her, he saw she was indeed breathing, a slow, steady breath of deep sleep.

"Hey, wake up!" Alex shook one of the men. The man groaned, fluttered his eyes, and fell back asleep, slumping to the ground.

Alex stepped back, stunned.

Dante had a bad taste in his mouth. This was unnatural sleep, like they were held captive.

"Look!" Sophia exclaimed. She carefully stepped over sprawled limbs.

Dante followed her with his gaze, curious. She knelt down to another sleeping body. He didn't understand what was different about this particular person. He glanced at Alex, who shrugged.

When nobody said anything, Sophia explained, "Don't you see? It's my mother!"

Dante hurried over to where she was, careful to not step on any limbs. In the torch's light, he recognized the golden hair, even though he didn't recognize the woman. *So this is Sophia's mother.* Her wings folded around her, like a feathery blanket.

"Mother, wake up!" Sophia said, reaching for her arm. She shook her shoulder. Her mother barely stirred. "Please, it's me! Please wake up!" Desperation crept into her voice.

"Why won't she wake up?" Dante asked.

"None of them will wake," Charon said behind him.

Dante turned around. Charon's face was solemn, and his eyes were mournful.

"But why?" Sophia's voice wavered.

"That's the way things are," Charon replied. A shadow passed over his eyes.

Dante looked back at Sophia's mother. She appeared perfectly healthy, only sleeping, as if at any moment, she would wake up and start talking.

"Will she sleep forever?" Sophia asked.

Charon shook his head. "They all will sleep until the end of time."

"Isn't that the same thing?" Dante asked. He hated riddles.

This time Charon stayed quiet.

Dante rubbed his forehead. Tiredness crept into his bones and he wondered how long he had been awake for. It was impossible to tell time in the dark cave.

"So is this better than the zombies?" he asked. "What do you think, Alex?" Dante turned to him, but he didn't see him. That instantly felt wrong. Dante's chest tightened. "Where's Alex?"

He held up his torch and circled around. No Alex.

"He couldn't have gotten far," she said but worry crept into her voice.

Dante knew she also felt that cold drop of fear—the fear of something wrong.

"He is right here," Charon said, hobbling on his oar-cane. He stopped at a sleeping body on the ground.

That can't be right. His heart pounded as he went over to him.

"Why is he sleeping?" Dante asked. He shook Alex, trying to wake him, but he knew it was too late already. Whatever spell all these people were under, Alex was, too.

"It is the nature of this place," Charon said.

Even as he said it, Dante felt the weariness take over him. His limbs felt heavy and his eyelids drooped.

"You'll soon see why this is the true Hell." Charon's eyes were dark.

Dante's knees sank to the ground. He could barely keep vertical now. His body was begging him to lie down, but he knew in his heart if he laid down, he would never get back up.

"Sweet dreams," Charon said as he turned back to his boat. "And good luck. You'll need it."

Dante sat back on his heels. His head swam, but he tried to keep afloat. He couldn't succumb to the seduction of sleep. His torch dropped and sputtered.

"Sophia," he said thickly. "Don't go to sleep." He looked over at her with effort. She was sitting with her legs folded underneath her. Her head was bowed, her hair hanging limply around her.

"Sophia," he said louder, trying to get a response.

She sank to the ground. Her wings opened and fluttered.

"Sophia!" he yelled. Desperation screeched in his voice.

His torch burned down, the light fading. It wasn't long until the darkness ate the last flicker of light. And then he could see nothing. Sleep and darkness were so overwhelming Dante could not fight it anymore. He felt the cold, hard rock beneath him as he sank down on the ground. Then he closed his eyes.

And he was asleep.

Chapter 29

Ryan was sitting next to Dante when he woke up. Blinking away the sleep, Dante sat up.

"Ryan! Oh, thank God you're okay," Dante said with relief.

"I've never been better." Ryan looked healthy and refreshed. There was even a glow about him.

"I'm sorry about your death. I wish there was something I could've done," Dante said.

"You're sorry I'm not still in Hell? You have a weird way of apologizing."

"But now you're stuck in Hades. I don't think this is any better."

Ryan shook his head. "I'm not where you are."

Dante looked around and realized there was a haze of light. "Where's that light coming from? It was so dark before."

In the dim light, Dante searched for Sophia and Alex but he couldn't see them. He couldn't see any other bodies, either. That stuck him as odd.

"Oh, this light won't last long," Ryan said. There was something cryptic in how he said it. It reminded Dante of Charon. *More riddles.*

"Where are you?" Dante asked in hush tones.

"In a better place," Ryan replied. "Because of you."

"I don't understand."

"Remember? You prayed for me."

The light was fading. He knew without understanding their time was ending.

"I still don't get it."

Ryan grew quiet for a few moments before answering.

"What's not to understand? You're a reaper. It's more than sending souls to Hell. It's sending souls to their next part of their journey."

Goosebumps traveled across his arms like a cold chill.

"What are you saying?" Dante asked.

But Ryan didn't reply. He couldn't. Right before Dante's eyes, Ryan started bleeding. Blood ran down the side of his face, pouring on his neck and chest. Ryan fell to the ground, his limbs at odd angles. The same way he last saw Ryan laying at the bottom of the cliff.

Dante's breath caught in his throat. He wanted to scream but he couldn't. He was stuck. All he could do was watch in horror.

He opened his eyes. His pulse thundered in his ears. He blinked but he couldn't see anything. He was back in Hades.

"Ryan?" he called out thickly. His tongue felt like it was being weighed down. The dark cave was eerily silent. So silent his heartbeat sounded as loud as a beating drum.

It was just a dream. Relief washed over him. It was terrifying to see Ryan like that. But if it all was a dream, then he never actually got to talk with Ryan. *I really hope he is in a better place. Maybe someday, I'll know for sure.*

***

He heard shuffling and a yawn. By that alone, he already knew it was Sophia. *She's waking up!* With renewed energy, he hurried to find his torch on the ground. A few seconds later, he had light. *Thanks to Ryan.*

Sophia sat up, rubbing her eyes.

Dante ran to her. "Are you okay? Try to stay awake."

She tugged at his sleeve excitedly with bright eyes. "I talked with my mother!"

He looked down next to her. Her mother was still sleeping in the same position as when he saw her last.

"Uh, that's great. Did she wake up, too?" He had misgivings after his own vivid dream, but he went along with it. He had never seen her so happy before.

"Yes! I told you, we were talking." Sophia sighed happily. "I never thought I would see her again, let alone talk to her." She gently moved the hair out of her mother's face. "Wake up and meet Dante." Her mother's chest rose and fell, but otherwise, it looked like she was dead. Dante gulped, hoping for Sophia's sake she really did talk to her.

"Oh, it's okay, don't worry about it," Dante said quickly.

He watched while Sophia kept trying to shake her mother awake.

"Mother, please wake up!" Her fingers tightened on her mother's robe, as if willing her to rise.

"Sophia," Dante said as gently as he could. "I'm not sure if you really talked with her. I think you might've dreamed it. I had a dream too and it was so real—"

"I did!" She cut him off so unexpectedly he jerked his head back.

"All I'm saying is that—"

"And I'm saying I really did talk to her!" She snapped.

"Are you sure?"

"I know you doubt me."

"It's just that I had a dream about Ryan. I thought I was really talking to him. I mean, I wish I really was talking to him, but it was only a dream."

"Fine, don't believe me. I don't care." Her voice frosted over.

"Remember what Charon said. It's the nature of this place. It's a cursed sleep."

"If this is the only way I can talk to my mother again, so be it." A tear fell down her cheek.

Dante's heart fell with it. "Sophia," he pleaded, but she turned from him.

She laid down next to her mother and closed her eyes. Soon enough, her breaths became deep and slow.

His throat tightened. Trying to escape Hell, being stuck in Hades, none of that was as bad as Sophia mad at him. *We've been through it all. Don't leave me now.*

He had to give her hope. Give her a reason to believe in his promise. *No matter what, we figure a way out of here.* Sleep continued to whisper sweet-nothings in his ears but he tried to shut them out. *I don't want to live in dreams. This isn't life. I didn't run through Hell to just succumb to sleep.* He wished Sophia wouldn't choose that path.

***

Everything was dark and quiet outside of his torch's light. And even the flame wasn't letting out much illumination. Its soft, warm glow only added to the soothing environment, much like a nightlight. And he was so tired. His eyelids slid down, but he yanked them back up. *I have to stay awake.*

Sandy-colored hair caught his attention. Snoring softly, Alex was curled up, his bangs hanging over his eyes.

Dante reached over and shook his shoulder. "Alex."

Alex groaned and pushed Dante's hand away.

"Alex, wake up," Dante said, louder this time.

Another groan.

"We need to get out of here." Dante shook Alex's whole body. "Get up."

"Go away!" Alex pushed him and rolled away. Snoring soon followed.

Dante sighed. He wasn't getting anywhere. He couldn't even keep Alex and Sophia awake. *What can I possibly do now?* He had no one to help him and no way of knowing how to get out of here.

Sleep. It called to him and pulled him down. His eyelids drooped. This time he didn't have the energy to force them back up.

***

He woke up in bed. In his own bed. He jolted up with a start. He hadn't seen his home in so long that it looked strange.

There was a knock at the door, and his mother appeared. She smiled at him as she tucked back a loose strand of hair.

"Morning," she said. "You need to get up before you're late."

Tears welled up at the sight of his mother in the doorway. Until now, he didn't realize how much he missed her and missed the life he had. Everything was so much simpler then.

He sprang out of bed and ran to her, pulling her into a big hug.

"What's all this for?" she asked.

"I miss you," he said, his throat tightening.

His mother chuckled. "I haven't gone anywhere. Now, don't be silly, you have work to do."

Right, I'm a reaper. He almost remembered something but it eluded him. He reached for his scythe at his back. It wasn't there. A memory bubbled closer to the surface.

"Your scythe is hanging up. Now hurry!" his mother shooed him to the front door. And indeed, his scythe was hanging right where it was supposed to be.

He lifted it off the hook and inspected it. It was his, alright. But something was wrong. He turned to his mother.

"I'm not a reaper anymore," he said.

She looked at him funny. "Of course you are."

"No, I'm not. I refuse to reap any more souls."

"You're a reaper no matter what."

"I don't want to be."

She stared at him, pursing her lips. "That's the purpose God gave you: to be a reaper. You can't forsake that."

"I can and I will," Dante countered, feeling determination rise. He didn't like the thought that being a reaper was his only purpose. He wanted to defy that destiny. Not wanting to hear more about it, he flung the front door open.

And the dark cave appeared before him. An odd feeling overwhelmed him. He was aware he was dreaming, yet the dream seemed so real. The light from the room spilled into the dark cave. In the stream of light, he saw himself sprawled out on the ground, sleeping. The odd feeling in the pit of his stomach intensified.

"Until you accept who you are, you will never escape," his mother said behind him.

He jumped and turned. He stared at her. "How do you know that?" he asked.

But she didn't answer.

***

Dante awoke with a start. *So I did fall back asleep.* He cursed again. He thought the hardest part was trying to stay awake. Now he realized the hardest part was knowing whether he was dreaming or not. His brain felt foggy and he shook his head as if that would clear it. He had to think of a way to clue him in. There had to be something he could do to test if he was actually awake.

With a groan, he sat up. Water dripped around him, echoing in the dark cave. But that wasn't the only sound. A steady splash of water filled the air as the sound came closer. An accompanying lantern followed it. Charon was back.

"Charon!" Dante called. He pulled himself up, wobbling on weak feet. His body fought him, wanting to go back to sleep.

"Take us back across! We'll pay you!" Dante didn't know if Sophia had any more coins, but Charon didn't have to know that.

Charon cackled as he swung the lantern toward the shore. His wrinkles were in sharp contrast from the bright light and deep shadows. "What's that? You're not having fun?" He laughed again as if he said something funny. "Aren't you supposed to be sleeping?"

Dante frowned in annoyance. "Now who's asking all the questions?"

Charon laughed again. "It doesn't matter. You'll give into sleep soon. They all do." He waved vaguely around him. The other souls in the boat looked around silently with confusion in their eyes.

"Don't come here!" Dante shouted at them. "Turn back now! Save yourselves!" He waved frantically as if that would do something.

Charon shook his head. "It's too late. They already paid their toll. Besides, why are you trying to save them when you can't even save yourself?"

His question made Dante pause. *Until you accept who you are, you will never escape.* What did that even mean? It was only a dream. All of his dreams were useless. They didn't help. All they did was confuse him.

He dropped his hands. Only then did he notice he was holding something. He felt a weird sensation in the pit of his stomach like he did in his dream. He never remembered having anything in his hands. Slowly, he brought his hand up, staring at it in the lantern's light.

At first, he didn't believe it. He must be dreaming again. But no, he felt the rough surface against his fingers.

It was his scythe. He lost it when he came to Hades. But now it was in his hand—he picked it up in his dream. *But that was just a dream.*

The scythe's blade glinted in the light. Dante stared at it if he could find answers within it.

If that was real, then what else was real? He questioned everything that had happened to him since he got here.

What was real and what was a dream?

Chapter 30

Charon rowed away and took the light with him. The lantern swung rhythmically each time he rowed. Its weak light dimmed to nothing once he reached the far shore.

And there he sat in the darkness. The chill creeping up from the river, sucking out any last remaining warmth. The only sounds were the endless breaths of cursed slumber.

I have to stay awake. He didn't know what he was supposed to do exactly, but he was determined to not fall asleep. Every time his eyelids felt heavy, he squeezed the staff of his scythe even tighter like it was his life-line. *How ironic.*

But it did give him an idea. Taking a big breath, he pressed his palm into his left eye. *Pain will definitely keep me awake.* But none came. He removed his head wrap and blinked his eyes. He couldn't see anything in the dark, but it didn't hurt. Even more, there wasn't any blood. It was like he never had a wound at all.

Heart racing, he checked his numerous other wounds. Nothing. He was perfectly healthy. *Is this because I died? The wounds I got in Hell didn't transfer?* His thoughts raced but his mind couldn't keep up. He rubbed his eyes. There was something more significant about this revelation, but in his foggy brain, he couldn't quite pick it out.

Sleep. Even rubbing his eyes was too much work. He dropped them, making his scythe clatter against the stones.

My wounds are gone. He clung to this knowledge. This was important. If only he could think straight. But he laid there, his eyelids fluttering. Each time his eyelids slid down, he struggled with all his might to lift them a fraction of an inch. They slid down even easier and farther the next time.

He was caught in a trance, not sleeping, not awake. It was a torturous struggle of being. *How long can I keep this up?*

Charon's lantern flickered in the distance. Soon enough, he could even hear when the oar hit the water.

Dante focused the lantern, pushing away the sleep that begged him to give in. Seeing light in this dark place gave him the needed boost of energy. He quickly stood before sleep could protest.

Charon pushed the boat closer to the shore with a strength that didn't match his frail physique.

"Okay, you're here," he told the couple in the boat. "Now get out."

The man and woman's eyes were wide with fear. "What do we do now?" the woman asked as they climbed out.

"Sleep," Charon cackled and turned away from them.

The man started to ask, but he slumped to the ground before a syllable could leave his lips. The woman screamed and rushed to his side.

"Help him!" she cried.

Charon didn't even turn toward her. He stood as still as stone.

But it didn't matter. She too keeled over in sleep, snoring loudly.

Charon didn't say anything and neither did Dante. He could only stare at the new arrivals, subjected to the same torment as the rest of them. Watching Charon doing his job brought back memories of his own time reaping souls. He realized they basically had the same job. Charon was caught in this in-between space of endlessly ferrying souls to their eternal slumber. Every time Charon picked up new passengers, he knew what was going to happen to them. As soon as the souls crossed the river and arrived on the shore, they would give in to sleep forever. Dante's heart twisted in pity. *What a lonely and miserable existence. Not even anyone to talk to.*

Dante focused his gaze on Charon. The lamp light flickered on Charon's face, but his eyes were shrouded in darkness.

"How can you still keep doing this?" Dante asked, shaking his head. "Don't you hate it?"

"This is my God-given duty," Charon replied in a matter-of-fact tone.

Until you accept who you are, you will never escape. His mother's voice echoed in his mind. *Was it really a dream?*

"You can stop doing it," Dante said. "I did."

Charon let out a sharp laugh. "And a lot of good it did for you. You were ostracized, cast into Hell, had the dumb luck of dying again, to only be another body snoring away for eternity. Please tell me how that was a good idea."

As Charon spoke, Dante's mouth opened but no sound came out. A chill crossed over him that had nothing to do with the cold.

"How do you know that?" Dante asked in disbelief. "There's no way for you to know all that."

Charon waved his hand as if shooing away the question. "Oh, people tell you a lot of interesting things while they're waiting to cross."

The light from the lantern caught Charon's eyes. They glimmered sharp blue with a rim of aged yellow. *They were the same eyes as that old reaper.* Dante's heart seized. *But that's impossible.* The thought was so preposterous that he shoved it aside.

"But why do it?" Dante waved his arms around, gesturing to the souls sleeping all around them. "This is an endless, horrible cycle. You already know how it is going to end. Why keep doing this?" A desperation pinched his voice. This was too close to home for him.

"I already told you," Charon said. "God wants me to carry out this duty, and so I will."

"Don't you hate it? You can't stand there and tell me this is what you want to do."

"This is all a part of His plan. I am fulfilling my part in it."

"But why would He create Hell?" Dante asked.

Charon didn't meet his gaze, looking at something only he could see. He was quiet for so long that Dante started to doubt if he said anything at all.

"Did you know cold doesn't exist?" Charon finally replied.

Goosebumps rippled up and down his arms. A chill pierced the back of his neck. He felt even more aware of the icy air than ever before.

"That's odd, because I feel cold right now," Dante said, shivering.

Charon shook his head so much that it made the lantern sway. "No, cold is the absence of heat."

"Isn't that saying the same thing?" *Is he talking in riddles again?*

"No, it's not. When you feel warm, you don't even notice it. That's your normal temperature of being. When you're warm, you're comfortable, happy, you can live your life, go about your day. But when you feel the absence of heat, all you can think about is how cold you feel and try whatever you can to get back to the warmth."

"Okay, that's true. But what does that have to do with anything?"

Charon looked sharply at him. "Don't you get it?"

Dante shook his head.

Charon sighed in frustration. He thrusted his oar into the ground and rested an arm on top of the handle. "Hell is the absence of God. Without God, there is only death. Without God, there is only suffering. Without God, what is left? God is good, so how can good exist without God? Only with God is there life. Only with God is there hope."

Hope. That one word rang brightly. He looked up. *Hope.* Could he dare to believe? For a moment, it gripped him. The mere existence of actual hope caught ahold of him. A fire burned inside of him, roaring back to life. To truly think he could escape this place.

A blanket of doubt smothered his mind. He blinked and the moment was gone. The fire fizzled into smoke, drifting away, leaving him feeling cold and empty.

"But it's too late for hope. We're already in Hell. How can there still be hope if God has abandoned us?" Dante asked.

Charon shook his head. "It is not God who has abandoned you but you who abandoned God."

"That doesn't answer the question. Besides, does semantics really matter right now? We're still in Hell regardless," Dante said.

Charon sighed and shook his head. "You haven't been listening to anything I said."

"What do you mean?" Dante scoffed. "I heard every word. You just aren't explaining anything."

Charon didn't say anything but shook his head, which infuriated Dante even more.

"What do you know anyway?" But Charon wouldn't reply. Anger built in his chest and came flooding out. "I want answers. I want to know why if God is so good, then why does He even allow suffering and death at all? Why does God have souls that He himself created be condemned to Hell? And don't give me the bullshit analogy of cold and hot. Why would He make my duty a reaper so I have to watch people die to only then send them to Hell? Why?" Dante's voice strained. The last word echoed around them and clung to the darkness.

Until you accept who you are, you will never escape. No, I refuse to. And I will get out of here no matter what. I know there is one person who can definitely answer my questions.

Dante got so lost in his thoughts he didn't notice until now that Charon had slipped back into his boat. The lantern swayed as Charon rowed away to the other side of the shore. Dante's heart sank as he realized Charon was carrying out his duty and bringing more unfortunate souls across. But the sight of it made Dante more determined.

He gripped his scythe. Feeling it in his hand made him more irritated. *How can this stupid scythe help now?* His dream with Ryan flickered into the forefront of his mind. *It's more than sending souls to*

Hell. It's sending souls to their next part of their journey. Okay, but this is where the journey ends, right? It's not like we can fly out of here.

His breath stopped, but his heart hammered in his ears, screaming at him.

It's not like we can fly out of here.

He pressed his fingers to his left eye.

My wounds are gone. His body shook with realization. *Does that mean Sophia's are gone, too?*

Sleep continued to whisper in his ear, but he pushed it away. The only light was fading as Charon was almost out of sight, but Dante knew where to go almost by instinct. He stepped over various limbs and stopped when he saw the last gleam of light reflected on golden hair.

"Sophia."

The light on her hair looked the same as it did that night when the moon was full. The same night that they whispered conspiracies by the fire while the hellhounds howled. The same night he made a promise to her.

"Sophia," he said louder.

She stirred but didn't reply.

"Sophia!"

She rubbed the tiredness out of her eyes.

"What are you doing?"

Dante smiled. "Keeping my promise."

Chapter 31

The light was completely gone, but Dante could still see Sophia's reaction in his mind's eye. He knew she was giving him a cold look by the silence.

"How? We're even further away from getting out of here than before." Her words iced the air.

"Listen," he said in a rush. "My wounds are gone, but what about yours?"

Sophia sucked in her breath. "Dante, stop. I don't know if I can keep doing this. With all your scheming and promises, I just don't know. I don't know how to get out of here. We died getting here, remember? We're in a place where even I don't know."

"We have to try."

"Do we? Why? Here, I'm away from my father, away from my cursed legacy. Here, I'm with my mother. I don't care if I can only talk to her in my dreams." Sophia shook her head. "What is your obsession with escaping?"

"You think I'm escaping? You're the one escaping. This is easy—just sleep your life away! That's not a life. Do you think your mother wants this for you?"

"Don't you dare bring my mother into this!"

"You're the one who promised her that you would go back to Heaven!"

"And what about your mother? Hmm? Does she want this life for you?"

"Well, obviously she doesn't want me to be in Hell," Dante faltered, remembering his dream. *You'll never escape until you accept who you are. How is being a reaper helping me now?* He shook his head, trying to clear his thoughts. *I need to focus on what's important.*

"Listen, Sophia, I think you can fly now! We can fly out of here!"

"Oh, I see how it is. You want me to go with you because I'm the only one who can fly, is that right? Because if I don't go, then you can't escape."

Her words pierced Dante's heart. "Why do you have to say it like that? Like I'm using you?"

"You are, aren't you? Why aren't you begging Alex to wake up and come with you?"

Dante bowed his head. "I haven't forgotten Alex. I will find a way to save him, too."

"Well, let me know because I'm not leaving my mother for your crazy schemes. Who knows what level of Hell we will end up on next!" Sophia lay down to fall asleep.

"Please don't leave me," Dante whispered. She was next to him yet she felt so far away.

"If you think you can escape, then do it on your own."

"This whole time, I've had nothing but this useless scythe and an impossible hope. But the alternative is so much worse. Look around! Do you really want to spend eternity here, in a cold, damp cave, caught in cursed dreams?"

"But what about my mother? How can I leave her?"

He looked over at Alex. "We'll come back for them. We'll find a way."

"Are you seriously making another promise when you can't even keep your first one?"

Reapers send people to the next part of their journey. I sent Ryan on. I don't know how I did it, but there has to be a way to do it for them too.

"Please believe me. Trust me like you once did. I need you. Not your wings, but you."

"I won't leave. Go without me."

In his mind, his path opened up to him. Against all odds, he was able to crawl and climb his way out of here, out of Hell. He was able to do the impossible, open Heaven's Gate and enter. Then what? To be surrounded by those he hated? Only to be cast out? Only to be sent back to Hell or worse, be forced to be what he hated the most—a reaper. Without Sophia, did he really have a reason? Even if he did all that, did he want to without her?

"You're right. Stay here, and I'll stay with you."

"What are you saying?"

Dante laid down. The torch spluttered and threatened to go out. Only a small flame still held out, but not for much longer. When the light goes out, that would be it. In his bones, he knew this time, if he fell asleep, he wasn't getting up.

"Dante, don't do this. Why can't you leave me? It's fine, really. I'll stay here. Go on without me. I know you really want to escape. Just go."

The flame grew smaller and the darkness pressed in, thick and black.

When he first fell, he felt so angry, bitter. He didn't feel any of that now. *Why do I want to escape? What am I trying to prove? What am I without being a reaper? Nothing. Who am I without Sophia? Nothing. Even Alex gave me hope when I had none. They both gave me hope. Without them, I am nothing.*

The flame was so small now. Only the barest hint of flame, more smoke than light now.

What is the use of escaping without them? There were more important things. He couldn't see that until now.

"You're right. I don't want to leave you and Alex. We've been together all this time. I don't want to be apart now."

She sobbed. "Why're you saying this?"

"I've been so focused on escaping, I forgot to focus on what's really important. How can I go on without you? Is that so hard to understand? I'll lay beside you for the rest of eternity. That doesn't sound so bad, does it?"

The flame flickered for the last time and went out in a puff of smoke. It was completely dark now. He shut his eyes, letting himself finally sleep without struggle.

"No, I can't do this. You have given me hope when there was none. It is my turn to return the favor."

Dante heard the distinct sound of wings fluttering. Wind whipped through his hair. And breathed life back into the flame. It roared back to life.

Dante opened his eyes.

She stood up. With a rush of wind, her wings unfurled and stretched. The white feathers caught the light and looked as if they were glowing too. Her wings spanned out, impossibly long.

He sat up, his heart pumping. He was used to seeing angels, but this felt different. She was downright *angelic*. She had never looked so beautiful. It was like he had never seen her before, as if this was her true form.

"Sophia, you're an angel," Dante said, feeling dumb as soon as he said it.

"So I wasn't before?"

"You know what I mean. You aren't a fallen angel. You are a real, actual angel."

Sophia's golden eyes brightened. "You really think so?" Her voice wavered like she wanted to cry.

"Yeah, and I would know," Dante replied. He smiled to himself. After all those years of hating angels and here he was, in the depths of Hell, with an angel who was his closest ally—his closest friend. Tommy and his other old friends flickered into his mind. *Yeah, she's even closer than that. We've literally been through Hell and died together. You don't do that and not feel anything for that person.*

"I've never met anyone like you, Dante. You deserve more than this. I still don't know if we can escape, but I'm willing to try. As long as I'm with you."

"But what about your mother?"

Sophia smiled. "Have you forgotten your promise already?"

"You really believe me?"

"I believe you will be the only one who can free my mother from this Hell."

Dante stood up. "I will free us all." The words vibrated in the air as if he said a vow.

He didn't know how but the flame wasn't just lit in the torch, it was lit in his very being. He gripped his scythe. *I don't know what it means to be a reaper. But I don't want to be nothing. If not for me, then for Sophia, her mother, and Alex. Maybe that is the secret. I was being selfish. If I have to be a reaper, then I'll do it for them. I can do it for them. If I did it for Ryan, then I know I can do it again. I don't know how but I know it's possible.*

Looking up, he still couldn't see what lay beyond in the depths of the darkness. He supposed that there was a high ceiling of a great, wide cavern.

The water quietly lapped onto shore. Dante let his focus shift down to the river. His eyes followed the water until it faded into black. *Charon will be back soon.* But Dante was done having conversations and riddles with him. *By the time he comes back, we'll be gone.* Determination rose in his chest and pumped through his veins. *I'll make sure of it.*

"We're getting out of here."

Sophia gazed at him, not saying anything right away. "You know, I've believed you every time you said that. And every time you say that, we get further and further away from where we started. Why is it different now?"

Dante nodded and stared right back at her.

"Because now, you can fly."

Sophia flapped her wings, trying them out. Big gusts of wind whipped through Dante's robes, smacking his arms and legs. She gazed at her newly-healed feathers.

"It's been so long. I thought I would never fly again," she whispered in awe.

"You remember how, right?"

She side-eyed him. "Of course. How could I forget?"

"Okay, but you are going to have to carry me." Dante didn't like the idea of Sophia having to hold him. He couldn't think of one kind of carrying position in which his pride wouldn't be hurt, but he had dealt with worse injuries.

"Like before?" she asked.

Dante blink, trying to remember. "Before?"

"Remember when we were escaping the city and I had to lift you up over the lava? How could *you* forget?"

Memories rushed back to him—the smoke and ash and heat. After everything that had happened, escaping a burning city didn't seem like a big deal anymore.

Dante nodded reluctantly. "Right. Yeah, like that."

She looked around. "But where am I flying to? How do we get out?"

"The same way the souls get here. We follow the water."

Dante glanced back. In the torch light, he could make out where Alex lay sleeping. Their faces were pale as ghosts and their chests barely rose and fell. *Were they really alive?*

He felt a twist of guilt. In his plan, he had to leave Alex behind. It wasn't right. But it was impossible to take him. Sophia could only carry one person. *I will make this right. One day, I promise I'll come back for them.*

He knelt by Alex and tried to wake him up. Alex grumbled but kept right on sleeping. No matter how hard Dante tried, Alex wouldn't wake up.

"Okay, fine then." He looked over at Sophia. *Maybe she really did talk with her mother in her dreams. Maybe I can still talk to Alex too.* He crouched closer to Alex. "Don't hate me, okay? I have to leave you. But I'll be back. I'll get you out of here. I'll find a way." His scythe felt heavy on his back. He freed Ryan by praying. Maybe he can pray for Alex, too.

Dante bowed his head. *Please forgive Alex. He has righted his wrongs. Have mercy on him.*

He watched as Alex continued to sleep. Unlike Ryan, Alex didn't disappear. He stayed where he was. *Then I'll come back.*

He turned back to Sophia. Her head was bowed, whispering to her mother. Telling her goodbye.

She got up and rubbed her eyes. He thought she was crying until she yawned.

"No, don't sleep now," Dante said firmly. "You have to stay awake."

"Aren't you tired?" she asked in a strained voice.

Dante shook his head. "Not anymore. I have a plan." His heart thudded with determination and anticipation. He was too riled up to sleep now.

Dante heard a splashing sound. Following the noise, he could see the twinkle of Charon's lantern. He cursed silently. They had spent too much time dawdling. It was time to go. In the corner of his eye, Dante saw Sophia yawn again. *If we don't do this now, we may not have the chance again.*

He grabbed her arm. "Let's go."

She looked into his eyes, searching. "You really will get us out of here?"

Determination was taunt in his chest. "I promised you, didn't I?"

Without another word, she scooped him up by his armpits. Like before, he was surprised at her strength. Her wings fell and rose with the wind billowing behind them. In a gust, his feet left the ground, dangling in the air. Below them soon became engulfed in darkness as they flew higher.

A cold splash of water landed on his forehead. From Sophia's glow, tips of stalactites shined like pointy fangs bearing down on them.

"Be careful not to fly too high," Dante cautioned. He watched another fang sweep right over his head.

"Okay, okay, but I can't see where to go." Sophia's voice was as tight as her grip on him.

"We need to see the water to follow it." He held out his torch.

Wings on each side of him flapped and outstretched into a glide. She dipped down, and Dante felt his stomach flop from the sudden shift in altitude. Soon enough, the torch's flames caught the wavering sheen of liquid.

"Now I see," she muttered. "But do you really think we can fly out of here? Didn't we technically die getting here?"

"Well, that's what Charon said. But he said that this was a different place called Hades. So, if this is a physical place, then there's a spot where it connects to Hell. And I don't think it was an accident that we 'died' when we fell down the waterfall."

"So this plan is hinging on that conjecture? Why does that not surprise me."

"Yeah, well, that's all I got." Dante tried to shrug, already forgetting that she was holding him.

"Hey, don't move around! I don't want to drop you," Sophia said, clenching him even tighter.

Dante thought he might be losing circulation from her holding him so tight, but he didn't say anything. He also didn't want her to drop him.

***

It felt like they had been flying like this for a while, but there was nothing to gauge the time. It could be minutes or hours. Dante had no idea. But it felt long enough for him to have doubts. It started as he watched the squiggly lines of light that illuminated the water below. So many lines of light they passed and it kept going. Why was it that every time he had a plan, it only got thwarted and then put him in a worse predicament?

Sophia gasped, knocking Dante out of his thoughts.

"It's the waterfall!" she exclaimed and flapped her wings harder.

It truly was. He could hear it more than see it. The rushing water roared in anger as it crashed into the river. As they swooped closer, he felt the magnitude of energy emulating off the falling water. Mist filled the air, making his skin cold and clammy.

Then they were going up. It was a great feeling. Not since they were climbing the mountain had he felt like he was really making progress. *Can I dare to hope?* His breath caught, afraid that even the wrong breath would turn his luck. Even Sophia didn't say anything. They both were quiet and intent on their destination.

A blinding light seared his eyes. Dante shut his eyes and instinctively put up his hands as cover.

"What is that?" Dante asked, annoyed. Even with his eyelids shut, light pierced right through.

Sophia laughed. A full-body-down-to-her-soul laugh. A laugh that you could only make when the fear that had been building up is finally released.

"It's the sun! The sun! Dante, we're out! We did it!" She landed on solid ground and gave him a hug. "Dante, you did it!"

He looked around, stunned. His eyes adjusted enough to see the surroundings. Wheat fields waved in the hot wind. A red sun burned in the sky. And smoke from a ruined city billowed.

"Yeah, but," Dante stammered. "We're back in Hell."

Chapter 32

It was probably the only time in recorded history when anyone would be excited to be in Hell. But there she was, jumping up and down with glee, twirling with delight.

"Um, Sophia, don't you want to get out of Hell?" Dante asked.

For someone who was always so composed, it was a weird sight to see. But not an unwelcome one. His lips turned up, watching her. *We really have been through a lot together. And it's not over yet.*

She paused in her twirling to look over at him. Her eyes were bright and her cheeks were flushed with excitement.

"But it's like you said—I can fly now. We can keep flying right out of here!" Sophia tugged on his sleeve. "So, let's go! What are you waiting for?" She turned and pointed to the mountains disappearing into the clouds. "We know what to do, we know where to go. It's so easy now!"

And it was. Dante couldn't believe how easy it was to escape Hades. And it will be so easy to escape Hell now. It almost made the whole experience seem trivial. But something felt wrong to him. *What was he missing?* He felt the looming presence in the back of his mind and closed his eyes to concentrate. He breathed, clearing his mind.

And then he could smell it. The scent of brimstone and ash in the wind. And they carried a message. A memory triggered: *"Throughout the years, I realized the best way to completely break someone's spirit was to give them hope,"* Lucifer said. *"Go ahead and plan your escape again. Maybe you'll make it farther next time before we pluck you back."*

Lucifer. His heart seized. *How could I forget? We had one small victory but really, what have we gained?* Dante's mind raced, trying to come up with a plan, searching for a way this could actually work. *Yes, we have wings to fly, but so do the other Fallen.*

A noise broke his concentration. Instinctively, he looked up. Without really hearing them, he already knew. It was an unnatural cloud that moved against the wind. Dark and unnerving, the cloud flew closer.

Fear struck him. "Sophia, get down!" Dante hissed, yanking her arm.

Sophia grimaced but followed. They crouched in the wheat field. Stalks rippled around them. The heat near the ground was thick and heavy. The wheat made him itch, but he resisted the urge to scratch. It might be too late. The crows may have already seen them. But he wasn't going to take any chances.

As the crows soared overhead, a hushed sob slipped out of Sophia's lips. Dante glanced over, being careful to not turn his head. The flush from her cheeks drained away until she was pale as a ghost.

"They've seen us," she whispered, eyes wide with fear.

"You don't know that for sure."

Dante watched the dark cloud turn toward the city ruins. It seemed hopeless—except it wasn't. He wasn't sure why, but he felt different now. Ever since he made his decision to talk to the one person who could answer his questions, he felt a sense of calm. He could see clearer now. Was this how it felt to have hope? Dante wasn't sure if it was hope exactly. But one thing was for sure—they were flying their way out of Hell.

"We need to leave now," he said.

Sophia brushed the tears from her eyes. "And this time, I'll succeed."

Next thing Dante knew, an arm grasped him around his waist and his feet were only touching air.

Dante had never been carried so much in his life. This was a very minor grievance compared to everything else that was happening right now, but still, his face flushed at the thought.

But the embarrassment melted away as the ground disappeared into the smog of dust and ash. Soon he was only surrounded by air and wings.

I am finally doing it. After all I've been through, I'm finally escaping. His heart felt like it might burst with happiness and excitement. He allowed himself to hope. To truly and fully feel the warm rays of hope. It flowed through his veins and flooded his mind. He could hardly comprehend that he was getting out of here.

I will escape Hell. He repeated it so often—to himself, to everyone. After a while, he didn't know if he truly believed it. But it was all he had to go on. And now, his persistence paid off.

Watching Sophia's wings fluttering through the sky, Dante was in awe. He couldn't stop looking around, taking it all in. It was what he wanted for so long. And it was finally happening.

He couldn't believe he was actually escaping. Even better, they were going to break into Heaven. He didn't forget why this all happened to begin with. It was because he didn't want to be a part of the system where souls were sent to Hell. He wanted to break the cycle. And now it was his chance.

A shriek cut through his thoughts. More followed, like a chorus off-key. The screaming came from everywhere as the wind whipped around the vibrations. Then he saw the Furies. They were headed straight toward them.

So we were seen. Fear gripped him as hard as he gripped his scythe.

"Dante, what are we going to do?" she asked.

Black wings stretched out as the Furies swooped down at them. Their sharp eyes narrowed with intent, spying their prey.

Dante gulped. "Keep flying. I'll fight." He sounded more confident than he felt.

The three winged-women surrounded them with whips in their hands. He shuddered as he remembered the sting of lashes on his back.

Not again. He swung his scythe in a wide arc. The Furies darted out of the way.

He tried to wind up his swing again, but it was a lot more difficult to do mid-air while being held by his armpits. The Furies swiftly closed in on them. Opening their mouths, they screeched as one. The horrendous shrieks pierced his ears like his head was splitting in two. He covered his ears. But by doing so, he accidentally let go of his scythe. Dread washed over him as he watched his only weapon plummet back to Hell.

A whip wound tightly on his left arm. He grabbed it and yanked it toward him, pulling the Fury too. The terrifying creature filled his field of vision. The Fury's mouth opened, fangs out. He punched her face, his knuckles slamming into her jaw. Screams filled the air, but it might have been him. His fist throbbed in pain.

With all his strength, he jerked the whip to the side. The Fury swerved into another one. They became a tumble of wings and fell away.

"If you keep thrashing around, I won't be able to hold on to you," Sophia said through gritted teeth. She readjusted her hold on him.

"Sorry, just trying to keep us alive," Dante replied.

The whip's lash loosened on his arm, leaving behind red welts. He grabbed the whip and found the handle. The last Fury raised her own whip.

He snapped his wrist, and his whip's lash struck. But so did hers. A searing pain like lightning struck his chest. The agony blinded him. Thunder cracked as the whip smacked his legs.

"Hold on, Dante!" Sophia shouted. Her wings flapped faster. "We're almost there!"

He barely heard her voice through the pain. The welts on his chest and legs burned. Only now did he realize he had let go of the whip. He cursed. *I can't believe I lost two weapons.*

The Furies regrouped and all three turned menacing eyes back on Dante. He frantically wracked his brain. *What can I do now?* Panic seized him. As one, the Furies flapped their wings and dove down together, straight toward Dante.

In desperation, he shoved his hands in his pockets. Out came the flint and steel. A moment of doubt flickered in his mind. *What is this going to do?* But they were so close now. Without thinking, he did the only thing he could do with flint—he struck it. The spark started out small, but it was picked up by the wind. The flame billowed for a split second before blowing out. But in that moment, the Furies swerved aside, taken by surprise.

"We're here!" Sophia said excitedly. She dove down.

There it was—Hell's Gate. The rods were red with rust. Iron spikes lined the top of the gate, piercing the sky. It rested at the edge of a cliff, where so many souls had fallen from.

"Do you know how to open it?" she asked as they neared it.

Dante glanced back. The Furies were almost upon them again. And something was flying behind them that he couldn't see.

The gate opened. Out popped a gloomy-eyed soul and a red-headed reaper.

"Tommy!" Dante said in disbelief. To see him after all this time made him laugh. "What timing!"

Tommy's eyes widened with shock. Even his freckles paled. "Dante!"

Sophia flew through the opening.

"Shut the gate!" she demanded.

The Furies screeched as they approached. Sophia landed and let go of Dante. He slammed the gate closed.

"What trouble have you caused now?" Tommy asked, amazed.

Dante swallowed, knowing they didn't have time to talk. "Nothing much."

Hell's Gate rattled, its hinges shaking loose. Dante leaned his whole weight on it. The force behind the gate was strong. Too strong. *I don't know if I can hold it back.* As the gate began to open, Dante dug in his heels.

"Help me!" he said over his shoulder. Sophia ran and held the gate. Tommy was frozen in place.

"Will you help me?" Dante asked, looking at him.

A shadow of doubt clouded Tommy's eyes. "What have you done?"

"I'm escaping Hell." Dante leaned more into the gate while tips of bat wings poked through the opening. The Furies shrieked through the bars.

"It doesn't look like you've escaped anything," Tommy said slowly.

Tommy still didn't move, but the distance widened between them.

Dante's throat tightened. "I thought you were my friend."

The gate opened more and the shrieks grew louder. The whole span of bat wings entered into Purgatory.

Tommy shook his head. "You've brought evil here. This is beyond me." He took a step back.

Dante's eyes glistened with tears threatening to fall. *Alex would've helped me. And would've said something snarky and sarcastic as he did it.* But he left him. He abandoned him in Hades and now he wasn't sure if he would ever see him again.

A new force blew open the gate. Dante went flying and landed face-first into the rocky ground. Jagged edges scraped his jaw and hands.

"I demand Sophia and the reaper. They are mine." The voice rang like a brass horn.

Dante looked up but he already knew. In the gateway stood Lucifer, tall and majestic. His white wings flew open.

Lucifer's smile twisted into a sneer. "And they are coming back with me to Hell."

Chapter 33

The sun was at Lucifer's back, illuminating his wings, tingeing them red. The red light—the one that always haunted Dante—spilled beyond the entrance and engulfed the ground. As it overtook the gray mist of Purgatory, the mist shrank back to the huge balance scale. It internally glowed like a beacon, the only thing to stand against the red gloom.

From here, Gabriel walked forth.

"Go back to where you came from," he warned. "You are not meant to be here. You are disturbing the balance of this place."

Lucifer glared at him. "Do you forget, Gabriel? I once sat with you and broke bread. Does that mean nothing now?"

Gabriel shook his head sadly. "No, not when you have broken the natural order."

"And what do you say of me?" Sophia spoke up. "I have been subjugated to Hell through no fault of my own. I have done nothing wrong. My only crime is being born in Hell."

She walked closer to him, with arms out.

Gabriel recoiled from her. "Lucifer has a daughter? How can this be?" He studied her. "I remember you. You tried to escape before."

He looked at Dante. "She is the reason why you were banished, yet you said she was innocent."

"And I still believe it. I've been with her the entire time and she's never done anything wrong. All she wants is to be an angel like you and all the others."

Sophia looked at Gabriel with hopeful eyes. Her hands clasped together in a silent plea.

Lucifer was quiet, watching. He even smiled to himself, an amusement only he understood.

"Whatever this is, none of this is right. Anything that has to do with Lucifer isn't right. Dante, why are you getting mixed up in this? No good can come of this."

Tears streamed down Sophia's face. "So you are saying you won't accept me? That I'm cursed to live in Hell for eternity?"

"I am sorry, but that's the way things have to be." Gabriel stood tall, like a barrier that wouldn't budge.

"No, no, it can't be true!" Sophia ran across the area to the other side where Heaven's Gate stood—very tall and very closed. She rattled the gate, crying. "Let me in, let me in! Please, I'm just like you!"

But it wouldn't open. She slid down, bowing on her knees, her hands gripping the bars of the gate. "It's hopeless," she finally whispered in the silence.

Lucifer smiled wider. "Do you see now, dear daughter? No other place will have you. Enough of this nonsense. You will come back with me to rule."

She grasped the gate even tighter. "Never! I will never go back!"

Dante's heart tore out of his chest. Fresh fire burned in his veins. *How can the angels decide how it is? Who are they?* "What right do you have to tell her no, Gabriel? I'm tired of all this. I didn't escape Hell just to deal with the same bullshit." He looked at Lucifer. "Aren't you tired of it, too, Lucifer?"

Lucifer cocked his head to the side. A sinister look creeped over him. "Indulge me. What are you proposing?"

"Are you seriously content with simply ruling in that forsaken city? Why be king of the ashes when you can have the Kingdom of God?"

"And you would want this?" Lucifer countered. "Why?"

Dante looked over at Gabriel and even Tommy, who shrank from his gaze.

"I'm tired of everything. If we go back to Hell, then everything will resume the way it was. Whatever that 'natural order' is. More souls will be sent to Hell. Angels will keep thinking they're better than everyone else. Then everything I've done was for nothing. And I wouldn't be able to keep my promise." He looked at Sophia. She was still crying.

"No, I can't have that! This is it. I'm done. I will break the cycle." Dante looked at Lucifer. "I want to tear it all down. No one will go to Hell if it doesn't exist anymore."

Lucifer laughed. "I love the way you think. I told you before, we are a lot alike." He laughed again and stopped suddenly. "Yes, let's burn it all down," he whispered in a dangerous voice.

Gabriel protested. "Dante, you don't know what you're doing!"

"I don't care," Dante said.

With a jerk, Lucifer threw his head back with his mouth open. A note struck the air. The very air vibrated. Dante felt it in his bones—his very soul.

Lucifer was calling the Fallen.

They appeared. All around, they flew like moths to the flame. They swarmed like a plague. He was surrounded by the Fallen. The last time there was a rebellion against God, they were sentenced to Hell, like Dante was. What will happen this time?

This is all my fault. Whatever happens, I started this. But I will finish it too. He remembered the angels who sentenced him here. *What will they say now? Maybe I can do it. I can break the wheel. Break the cycle.*

"Today is a new dawn," Lucifer declared. His white feathers glowed pink in the light of the red sun. "Today, we will take back what is rightfully ours. And I will sit on the throne of the Kingdom of Heaven!"

They all rose and flew to Heaven's Gate, where Sophia still knelt. She looked tearfully at Lucifer.

"Why are you sad? After all this time, we are together, as we should be. Yes, I should have listened to you. This time, we will break into Heaven together!" Lucifer opened his arms. "Now stand, Sophia Morningstar!"

She was quiet for another moment and then a small smile appeared on her lips. Purposely, she stood up.

"So nothing stands in our way," Sophia said. There was something regal in how she said it and Dante reminded himself that she was, in fact, royalty.

"Except this gate." Dante stepped forward. Being so close made his heart beat faster. This was the moment of truth. This is where everything has led to. He was aware of all the fallen angels gathered around him, not to mention Lucifer himself. And even Sophia. He hadn't completely fulfilled his promise yet. Not until they step inside the gate.

Heaven's Gate was towering. The golden rods of the gate were spaced out so much that he could definitely squeeze through. But he had a feeling it wouldn't be that easy.

His eyes locked on the gate. He had never been this close to the gate before. Angels wouldn't allow reapers to enter since they were apparently tainted with sin. Being reminded of it made his blood burn. *This is exactly why I'm breaking it all down. For shit like this.*

Dante reached his hand out. His hand almost touched the metal. Its golden glow shined on his fingers. Even the reflected light felt warm and soft. An ache for something he never knew and never had grew in his chest.

Until you accept who you are, you will never escape. The words echoed in his mind as loudly as if his mother was standing right next to him. *But I did escape.* A doubt wiggled and wormed in his mind. An odd feeling twisted in his stomach. *See? I'm doing exactly what I want to do.* But his words fell flat like he was trying to make himself believe it.

How can I be a reaper anymore? I don't have my scythe. The last time I saw it, it was falling back down to Hell. A new voice, stronger and clearer, rang in his mind. *Because it is time for your new one.*

Dante opened his eyes. His heart pounded. That voice wasn't his own. It wasn't echoes of memories. Something or someone talked to him. He stared at the gate as if it was going to answer his questions. *No, the questions can only be answered from inside.*

He grabbed the gate. He felt the resistance and pushed. And it opened.

Chapter 34

The gates of Heaven swung open. Nothing impeded him this time. And yet, Dante stood there. His hand was still outstretched. He blinked, not understanding.

"How did you open it?" Sophia asked.

Dante knew it was locked. He watched Sophia rattling the gate. But yet, at his touch, it opened. Something inside of him grew warm, as if the golden light from the gate had been absorbed into him.

After all these years, he saw what lay beyond the gates of Heaven. A golden path laid before him, inviting him in. The sun shone. Not an angry, red sun that scorched his face. This sun's rays bathed every surface with a golden, warm light. It sparkled on the golden bricks. His eyes followed the path to a tree on the riverbank. The tree was tall and sturdy with its thick branches reaching into the sky, grasping the warm light. Plump fruit hung heavily, weighed down by its own juices. Dante's stomach rumbled just looking at it.

Everywhere he looked, it was lush and green. Plants, shrubs, flowers, trees—everything grew in its full glory. Vibrant colors overwhelmed his eyes and a sweet, succulent aroma filled his lungs.

And in the distance, there it was—the Kingdom of Heaven. Its pearly white walls rose high into the air. As he looked at it, he felt a pull in his chest. *This is where I need to go.* He took a step forward.

A laugh stopped him in his tracks. Dante was so overwhelmed at the sight he forgot about the Fallen.

Lucifer threw his head back and laughed maniacally. It was a laugh where nothing was funny. It was a laugh filled with icy malice, like he was so filled with spite that it spilled out of him.

It froze Dante to his core. The cold realization chilled his bones. *I made a mistake. I shouldn't have brought Lucifer here. I should've found another way.*

Lucifer threw open his arms and addressed the white walls. "I have returned! You thought you could get rid of me! Hell cannot contain me, no gate can stop me! And this time, I will rule the Kingdom! Nothing will stand in our way. We are the Fallen!"

At his words, the Fallen cheered. Their voices were shrill and ear-piercing.

Dread was so palpable that it felt like lead in Dante's veins. He looked over at Sophia and met her eyes. Her face was drawn tight.

The Fallen were still screaming with spiteful delight. But as Dante watched them, the golden bricks beneath them turned black. His eyes widened. The lush green plants withered and curled into dry husks. Even the golden light dimmed around them like a giant shadow.

Their voices died down, their arms dropped to their sides. An unsettling hush passed over everyone like the calm before the storm.

Dante looked up. It wasn't his imagination that it got darker. There were angels—a lot of them. So many that they blocked the sun. A lightning bolt struck, searing cracks in the sky. Thunder rumbled and shook the ground. Dante stumbled, not expecting the severity of the shaking. It was like Heaven itself was angry at the intrusion.

"Why is everything turning black with ash?" Sophia asked, confused and even a bit sad.

"It's the manifestation of sin," Dante said. *So what the angels said was true.* He wanted to be angry, but he agreed with Sophia. He felt heavy with sadness too. *So I really don't belong here.* It was a hard pill to swallow. *This whole thing was a mistake. Maybe I should leave before it gets worse.*

Black spots appeared before his eyes. He blinked, but they were still there. They hovered and floated. As his field of vision widened, he realized they were everywhere. *It's ash.* It was like all the ruins and rubble followed them here. For a second, he was transported back to Hell, like a part of him was still there, shifting through the wreckage. *Have I truly escaped?* It didn't really feel like it. Yes, he was in Heaven. But it wasn't over.

A speck of ash glided along an invisible wind and alighted on a leaf. Instantly, the leaf and the whole plant shriveled up at its touch.

"I have unleashed a plague," Dante said, more to himself than anyone else. He was so angry he wanted to tear everything apart. But seeing the destruction up close—the destruction that he himself had caused—made him realize that he didn't really want that. Guilt dragged him down with its weight.

"My mother would be horrified to see what we have done. She wanted me to see the beauty of Heaven—not destroy it! We have to stop this, Dante. Before it's too late," Sophia said.

Dante looked down at the ash clinging to his feet and robes. Bile rose in his throat. *I'm the reason why Heaven is disintegrating.*

I wanted to tear it all down. But not like this. This is wrong. All around them, swirling like a black cloud, ash wafted in the wind, destroying everything it touched. Golden light dimmed. Soon, Heaven would look like Hell, and then what would be the difference? Charon's voice echoed in his mind. *Hell is the absence of God. Without God, what is left? God is good, so how can good exist without God? Only with God is there life. Only with God is there hope.* He froze. *Is this what Charon meant?*

"You are trespassing! Turn back now, or face the full wrath of Heaven itself!" Angels boomed overhead, sounding like thunder themselves.

Lucifer stepped forward and the ground blackened around him. "I will never back down. This is ours now!"

An archangel flew down closer to Lucifer. "You will never take over the Kingdom of God. You won't even take one more step." The archangel threw a golden spear. It soared through the air, appearing like a ray of light. Lucifer side-stepped out of the way before it pierced the ground.

Dante watched him. *I should've never joined forces with Lucifer. Gabriel was right. Nothing good can come of it. But what can I do?* The white walls of the kingdom caught Dante's eye. Despite the gloom around him, they still sparkled in the distance. *There's only one person who can answer my questions.*

"I need to talk to God and I'm not leaving until I do." He didn't know if he could demand that. But that was the only strong urge he felt. He was fixated on that one goal and he wouldn't stop until he did.

"You have no right, no authority to make any demands," the archangel declared. "You are our enemy, the same as these fallen angels. Justice will be swift." Quick as lightning, he hurled another spear of light. This time it was aimed right at Dante. His heart skipped a beat and every muscle screamed at him to move. He lurched forward as the spear soared behind him. The ground trembled as it made contact.

An idea struck him and he pulled out the spear. It was hot in his hands like it was a sun ray that had hardened. But now he had a weapon. *Let's not drop this one.*

Another spear whizzed through the air right at him. With his spear, he knocked it out of the way with a clang.

"Stop this now, reaper! Your presence is destroying Heaven!" the archangel said.

Dante breathed, inhaling ash. "But why? Why can't I be here?" His voice was raw. "And don't say it's because I'm tainted with sin."

"Are you blind? You're disrupting the balance."

"But why does it have to be this way? Why does everything hinge on the fact that humans sin?"

"It's the natural order. Why can't you accept that?"

"No, that's not a good enough answer." The questions burned in his veins. *I need to stop wasting time. I need to talk to God.*

"Get out of my way." Dante fumed.

"I cannot let that happen." The archangel stretched out a golden bow, the arrow glinting in the light.

Dante dodged. He staggered but he didn't fall. A hand held him steady.

"Come on," Sophia said, pulling him vertical. "We need to hurry before there's no Heaven left."

"Are you okay with this?" he asked.

"If we explain ourselves to God, then He can fix this, can't He? He *is* God, after all."

That made sense. Now, how were they going to get there alive? *There's no way Sophia and I can do this alone. We need help.*

The archangel readied another arrow. His eyes pierced Dante, and Dante had no doubt that his arrow would do the same. *I can't keep dodging forever.* He hurled the borrowed spear. But he never used a spear before and it showed—the archangel didn't even need to move.

Dante broke out in a cold sweat. *I'm out of options.*

Lucifer lunged at the archangel. In response, the archangel released the arrow but it only embedded itself in the dirt. Lucifer didn't miss his mark. His fingers seized the archangel's throat. Gasping, the archangel struggled as his wings faltered. Together they fell in a tangle of wings when they hit the ground.

Lucifer got up. The archangel didn't. And by the way he laid, he wasn't going to any time soon.

Dante hated himself for thinking it, but he needed Lucifer's help. *I need to get to God. And I will use Lucifer to do it.* It sounded backwards but he didn't have time to think about it.

Lucifer turned on Dante and choked him with an iron grip. "So are you with me or against me?"

Dante gritted his teeth. "We're going to the same place, right?"

"I will sit on the throne of God!"

"Okay...then, I'm going with you."

Lucifer seemed satisfied with that answer—at least enough to release him.

Dante gagged and rubbed his throat.

"Now tell me, reaper, how do you suppose we do that?"

Dante's eyes darted around as he desperately tried to come up with a plan. Everywhere he looked, someone wanted him dead.

Time was running out. And so was his luck.

Chapter 35

In a flurry of feathers, the Fallen began to rise into the sky. But the angels and archangels already flooded the heavens. Spears and arrows rained down on them. Many of Fallen's wings were quickly pinned down. They screamed in agony and crumbled to the ground, disappearing in a cloud of ash. A few Fallen broke through the ranks. They lunged and attacked angels.

Dante felt exposed with nothing to protect himself from the onslaught of angels. Sophia shrank closer to him. *We need to go, but where?*

Sophia pulled Dante aside. "You really want to help him?"

"Just until we get to God. I can't fight off all the angels of Heaven and Lucifer."

"Fair enough. But now what?"

The gardens gave way to a field of golden flowers. The gold sparkled and shimmered from each petal. It reminded him of the wheat fields in Hell. *We can take cover there.*

"There's no other way. Run for it!" He grabbed Sophia's hand and bolted for the field.

Lucifer and the rest of the Fallen followed at their heels.

***

The other day, Lucifer tried to kill them. Now, Lucifer was the only reason he wasn't dead. Dante couldn't get over the fact that he was shoulder to shoulder with the devil himself. *We're not on the same team. It's a temporary convenience.* He tried to console himself, but it didn't make him feel any better. It didn't help that as they ran, the world fell apart around them, exploding into ash.

They were a tornado, destroying everything in its path. Grass withered beneath his feet. Flowers and leaves wilted while ash swirled in their wake. Dante was sick at the sight.

Instead, he focused on the impossibly tall white buildings. With every step, he drew closer. *I have to make it. I have to.*

The fields helped to hide them, but he forgot one important difference—the ash signaled to anyone above where they were. At least the ash clouds obscured where they were exactly, so it wasn't a complete failure.

Spears and arrows barraged them with a few finding their mark. Even Lucifer had an arrow sticking out of his shoulder blade. Regardless, they kept running.

Angels swooped down for a melee attack. But they quickly veered away when ash accumulated on their wings and weighed them down. Then they stayed at a distance, defaulting to spears and arrows.

After a few close calls with nicks to prove it, Dante learned to run in a zigzag pattern to dodge the pointy death sticks.

"Can't you do what you did to the City of Dis?" Dante asked. He had seen the damage Lucifer could cause. *Why isn't he using his powers?*

"Have you learned nothing from me? Let the angels think they can best us—think they have us beat, running with tails between our legs. Let them think that," he smiled as another arrow embedded in his back. "All the better to crush them at the most opportune time."

Fear pricked Dante's neck. *I hope I'm not making a mistake.* Soon, they would have to split ways. *Yes, at the most opportune time.* A spear slammed down in front of him. *Which was not now.* He kept sprinting but his energy was depleting.

Dante breathed hard. The ash burned in his throat, making him cough. When they first broke into Heaven, the ash were only specks, but now clouds billowed around them. It seemed that the closer they got to God, the worse it got.

The fields ended abruptly. Before them emerged the Kingdom of Heaven. The gleaming white structures soared to the sky. Gold bricks lined the walkways, each perfectly fitted next to the other. Plants and vines grew everywhere as if the buildings were nestled in a garden.

As they raced into the kingdom, buildings gave way to plazas with elaborate mosaic designs inlaid with gems that glittered in the sun. Magnificent fountains sprayed water in the air, sounding like music to his ears.

He finally understood what Sophia's mother had written. Indeed, the City of Dis was a pale comparison to the Kingdom of God.

***

Dante stole a glance skyward. He expected to see something whizzing toward him but nothing. Everyone was scattered—angels and Fallen alike—all caught in their own skirmishes.

They ran further to the center of the kingdom when Lucifer stopped.

He whipped around to Dante, eyes narrowing. "Now it is time," Lucifer said. Another prophecy had been foretold.

Lucifer flew into the air, straight above, blocking out the sun. He slowly raised his arms. A light illuminated him as if he became a new sun, but this one was eerie and strange.

Dante gulped. He looked at Sophia. His fear reflected in her eyes.

"We're not safe here," he said.

The ground trembled beneath them.

"We need to get off the ground before the buildings come crashing down on us." She wasted no time and picked him up. No embarrassment flashed through him this time. They were too close to danger to have petty emotions.

Leaves slapped his face as they rose through the foliage. Buildings whizzed by. And soon, his feet brushed the tops of roofs. The clear sky opened up before them. Even at this height, the Kingdom of Heaven still looked impressive.

"But where's God?" Sophia asked, hovering.

Dante's eyes darted around. One building stood out, extra big and shiny.

"That's where I need to go," Dante said, pointing.

Sophia's wings fluttered as she caught an updraft. "Then let's hurry!"

Her wings beat faster and the wind rushed around him. It wasn't fast enough. An angel appeared before them. Sophia lurched back.

"Not any further! You are not worthy to be here."

"I'm not giving up now," Dante said.

The angel gave him a stern look. "You have caused enough trouble. It's over."

But I'm so close. Dante clenched his fists. "No, it's not."

The angel raised a spear of light. "But it is."

Sophia flew to the side to avoid it, but a flash of light filled his field of vision. A searing pain tore into his shoulder. Sophia screamed. Wind whistled in his ears as the pull of gravity overtook him. Dante's eyes widened with fear. *I'm falling.* He clasped at the air while the world blurred around him.

Chapter 36

Dante opened his eyes. There was a soft light that was everywhere but illuminated nothing, like it was so subdued that even surfaces couldn't reflect it. The sound of water was quiet and soothing. Something gently pushed against the water and the surface below moved in response. A suspicion crept into his mind. He sat up and the boat rocked. Dante frowned.

A familiar cackle came from behind him, but he didn't need to turn around. He already knew.

"Charon," Dante said with gritted teeth.

"And you thought you could escape." Charon laughed.

"Am I dead again?" Dante asked, annoyed. *Is that why Charon is here? Because he's my reaper?*

Charon laughed even harder. Dante's frown deepened.

Something was different. Before, it was so pitch dark that even Charon's lamplight couldn't pierce the darkness. Now they were surrounded by a faint glow, but Dante still couldn't see anything clearly. The light was like a mist that hovered around them.

Dante felt his frustration rising. "Tell me what's going on!"

Charon dipped his oar into water. "You are quite the troublemaker, Dante. Lucky for you, God isn't done with you yet."

"Wait, what do you mean?" Without even understanding why, he felt his heart racing. *God isn't done with me? When did he start?*

The boat glided and bumped into something. Dante lurched forward as the boat rocked.

"We're here," Charon said.

The misty light gave way to a set of stone stairs leading upwards. The top step disappeared back into the light.

"What's 'here'?"

"Go." The word had a finality to it. Chardon was done with questions and conversations.

With a sigh, Dante climbed out of the boat. He looked back at Charon, but he was gone, lost in the light.

He turned back to the stairs. Nothing moved but there was an air of expectation. He let out another breath. It felt like his heart was lodged in his throat.

There was nothing to do but go up. He started to climb with slow, purposeful steps. Even as he ascended, the top didn't seem like it was getting any closer. The stairs were endless. There were no landmarks to denote he was moving forward. *Is this some cosmic joke? Oh great, it's like Sisyphus. This is my punishment for cheating death. But instead of pushing a boulder up a hill over and over again, I'm climbing these stairs forever.*

He realized the pain in his shoulder from the angel's spear was gone. *If that even really happened.* He wondered where Sophia was right now. *Wherever she is, I hope she's ok.*

He lifted his leg to climb another step but there weren't any more stairs. *When did that happen?* Everything was so surreal. Slowly, he dropped his leg. And then he stood there, looking at a door.

The door was solid and shut. There were no adornments. It felt rigid without even touching it. *What's behind this door? Do I want to enter?*

He stood there. He knew he would open it. There wasn't much else to do. But he was trying to mentally prepare himself for what lay ahead. He felt a pull in his chest, the same sensation as he felt before.

He sucked in his breath and pushed the door open.

***

It opened to a great hall. Everything was an impossibly pure white—the floor, the walls, the columns. At first he couldn't understand it but as his eyes adjusted, he realized there were no shadows—only light. The columns lined each side of the walls, stretching high to an impossibly high ceiling. Looking up, he felt so miniature, so small like he was a drop of water in the whole ocean. The feeling washed over him. It was so strong that it felt like he was drowning.

His eyes followed the rows of columns to a tiered platform. He wasn't the only one here. There were hundreds of angels and souls adorned in all white. They all surrounded the platform on their knees and with heads bowed toward the center.

He suddenly felt self-conscious, standing there like he was intruding. He didn't want to even breathe because it was too noisy. Not to mention how haggard he must look. Everyone else was dressed in flowing, glossy white robes while his black robe was dirty, stained, and torn.

The longer he was in the space, the more he realized it wasn't actually silent. They were praying. All their voices blended together and echoed throughout the hall, creating a hum that vibrated everywhere. It resonated in his heart, his bones, his soul.

He took a shaky breath. *It's God.* His heart raced and a wave of dizziness washed over him, making him stumble. He breathed, trying to regain his thoughts. He didn't understand how he was here or why. But he needed to make the most of it. *I have questions to ask Him.*

He raised his eyes, following the steps of the platform. It rose higher and higher. His eyes began to water. He tried to keep looking up, but his mind began to swim. It was like a tidal wave. His breath caught. The sheer power was overwhelming. He never felt such a powerful force. He had been face-to-face with angels, archangels, fallen angels, and even Lucifer himself. Nothing could compare. To think Lucifer had any real power at all was laughable. Lucifer's power wasn't even a shadow compared to the awesome force of God.

He couldn't even look at Him. God's energy was so mighty that Dante couldn't even see Him. It was like trying to look straight into the sun. By just trying to made Dante fall to his knees. He closed his eyes, but the feeling followed him. He could still feel the force surrounding him. His body shook and his eyes watered even more.

I'm sorry. He didn't say it out loud but he knew God could hear him. *I'm sorry for everything.* His heart wrung with guilt. *I was foolish, stupid. I shouldn't have led the Fallen here.*

His eyes were still closed but somehow he could see a warm glow.

A voice that wasn't his own spoke in his mind. It was an odd feeling to hear a voice, not with his ears but within his own head. *Why are you here?* The question was stated in such a way that Dante felt that God knew but He wanted to hear Dante say it.

I need answers. I want to know, to understand.

What do you want to know? The voice sounded authoritative and patient, like a father talking to his young child.

All the questions sprung up in his mind. They jumbled around, overlapping each other. Memories passed through his mind. Images appeared and faded. Overwhelmed, Dante wasn't sure where to start.

God was quiet, as if He was waiting.

Moments passed before Dante settled on his first question.

Why haven't I met You before?

I have always been here. The door was always open for you.

Why did I have to go to Hell?

For some, they have to experience darkness before they see the light.

But You abandoned me.

I never have. I was always with you. I was the one who straightened your path, guided you.

What about all the sinners sent to Hell? Did You abandon them?

The door was always open for them as well. They chose to ignore it and go down a path of darkness.

You created them. Why do You want to see them suffer?

If only you knew how much it hurts to see their agony but you would not be able to bear the pain.

Why even give them the choice? Can't You make them follow You?

Humans are made in My image. I have given them the power to choose. Just like you. You are a child of God. You were created for a purpose. It is up to you whether or not you wish to fulfill that purpose.

But I don't want to be a reaper. I can't bear to send people to Hell for the rest of my life.

Being a reaper is more than that. A reaper merely escorts people on their next part of their journey. Death is not an ending but the beginning of another journey. I know you are well aware of that.

But still. This whole thing started because I don't want to be a reaper. I don't want to send sinners to Hell forever. I don't care if they deserve it. I can't do it anymore.

We are not on opposing sides. I created you. My will is your will. What you truly want will be offered to you.

What I truly want?

Dante was quiet for a moment. He escaped Hell, broke into Heaven, and got answers from God Himself. What now? *What do I truly want?* More memories passed through his mind and landed on the answer.

I want to save the souls trapped in Hell. I know they deserve it. But do they all need to stay for an eternity? Haven't they been punished enough? I want to free Alex, Sophia's mother, and others.

And you will have the power to do this, according to My will.

I can do that?

You always could. Now, go back and collect those who have redeemed themselves.

But I thought they had to be in Hell for eternity?

What is an eternity? What concept of time are you referring to? Time is not a line but a circle, a cycle.

There was a silence. In its place, a strong sensation in his whole body. Peace overcame him. Anger and bitterness left him. He felt the light glowing inside of him. He breathed, basking in the warm presence.

I'm ready. What do You want me to do?
Open your eyes.

Chapter 37

The light was blinding.

"Dante, I thought you were dead!" Sophia exclaimed.

He blinked, waiting for his eyes to adjust. "I was."

Groggily, he rose to his feet and glanced at her. Her mouth was agape.

"What's wrong?" he asked, confused.

"You—you have wings," she stuttered in surprise, pointing to his back.

His wings fluttered in response. It was a weird sensation.

Then he felt the weight. A weight that hasn't been there for a long time. He reached back and lifted a scythe off of his back.

It wasn't his. At least, it wasn't the same one as he had before. This scythe was gold. It looked like the same gold as the bars on heaven's gate. The ache for something he wanted and never had was replaced with a sense of peace and purpose.

The soft metal quickly warmed in his hand. He angled the scythe's blade, watching it catch the sun's rays. Gold wasn't ideal for fighting or harvesting. But it would do perfectly for reaping souls.

"What does this mean?" Sophia asked, leaning forward.

"I am a reaper," Dante said simply. "So it's true. In the end, I have accepted my duty as a reaper."

Her eyebrows furrowed. "But you hate reaping."

"I'm not sending souls to Hell. Instead, I'm saving souls. So I'm still a reaper. But in the way I want to." *No, the way God wants me to. But really, it's the same thing.*

She shook her head. "I don't understand. And how do you have wings?"

Lightning cracked, making them jump.

"I'll explain later. This isn't over," Dante said, eyeing the sky.

Angels, archangels, and the Fallen were a hurricane, swirling above them. It was a blur of fighting. In the eye of the storm, Lucifer hovered. Lightning splintered around him, and thunder shook the ground.

Dante tightened his jaw. "I have to stop him."

"Can you?"

It was a fair question. He wasn't sure either. But he started this mess and he had to fix it. And now he had something he didn't have before. Hope. Yes, he had a shiny new weapon and the wings were definitely convenient. But hope was more than that. With hope, all things were possible.

***

He spread his wings and flapped them. The air swirled around him, but his feet remained firmly on the ground.

"It's best not to overthink it. Focus on where you want to go and the wings will do the rest," Sophia coached.

Sucking in his breath, he tried to take her advice to heart. *I need to get to Lucifer.*

Air whistled in his ears as he lifted off. Eyes wide, he realized he actually did what she said. Wings glided in his peripheral vision. Sophia smiled. Now, they flew side by side to the midst of the battle. It felt weird to be flying, yet it was natural, too. As long as he didn't think about it too much, his muscles did the rest.

Lightning tore the sky apart, and the air crackled around him. In the center of the storm was Lucifer. *Wherever he is, destruction follows.* Dante flew closer. *I have to end this.*

"Stop this now, Lucifer," Dante said with conviction in his voice.

"I thought we went through this already. We're together now."

Dante shook his head. "I have learned one thing from you."

"And that is?"

"'Nothing is worse than almost getting everything you want and then having it snatched away from you at the very end,'" Dante quoted Lucifer.

Lucifer grimaced as his own words were shoved back in his face. "Oh, I see. You think you're being clever. But you have nothing to back those claims."

With his scythe, Dante struck a hole in the ground. Even though he was in the air, the scythe worked like a bolt of lightning that struck the ground. A chasm opened, gaping like a blood red scar.

"You forgot one thing, reaper. Hell's down there, and I'm up here." Lucifer laughed out of spite.

Dante's face burned but he held firm. *He may have a point, but it's not over yet. And I'm not the only one here who wants him gone.* He hoped the angels would do what should have been done to the Fallen the first time—what had been already done to the reapers.

An archangel flew in front of Lucifer, his six wings spreading out in a circle.

"Enough of this nonsense. You are banished from this sacred ground, now and forever." He waved his arm. "You have lost your wings. No longer can they aid you in such foolishness." As soon as he was done speaking, Lucifer's and all the Fallen's wings disappeared.

"Begone!" the archangel commanded.

As Lucifer started to fall, he sneered at Dante. "Don't think you're safe from me now."

Dante didn't say anything. Instead, he calmly waved goodbye.

They screamed as they descended to Hell. Dante shook his head. *No matter what, they always scream.*

The ash started to lessen. Without the Fallen, Heaven was already repairing itself. He looked down at his feet but no ash swirled around him. He breathed a sigh of relief.

"And you!"

Dante's eyes snapped up. There was something in the voice that he knew he was being addressed.

"It was you who allowed them entry! You will pay for your crimes!"

Dante brandished his golden scythe.

"Do you mean to fight?" the archangel asked.

Dante looked at Sophia. A moment passed between them. A sparkle gleamed in her eye and he knew she understood.

"No, I willingly go to Hell," Dante replied.

"And what of the fallen angel?"

Dante asked Sophia, "I'm going back to Hell to save your mother and Alex. Will you come with me?"

She didn't answer right away but instead flew closer. She placed her hand on top of his. "I've followed you to the depths of Hell and through the gates of Heaven. I'll follow you wherever you go."

She leaned closer. His heart skipped a beat. He felt the warmth of her breath and the softness of her lips as she kissed him.

"Then be off!" The archangel said. His voice was shrill. "Reaper, I never want to see you here again."

An old anger flared within him, but now it was only an echo. The sense of peace rose in its place.

Dante smiled. "I go where God wills it."

He took Sophia's hand. They didn't say anything else, but they didn't need to.

They fell—together.

About the Author

Ella Cutich has always been the dreamy, creative type. Her daydreams fuel her art and spark inspiration for stories. Even though she's known to be a little odd, she's finally come to terms with it. Wings & Scythe is her debut.

For more oddities, follow her on Tiktok and Instagram; both handles are @ellacutich.

Don't miss out!

Visit the website below and you can sign up to receive emails whenever Ella Cutich publishes a new book. There's no charge and no obligation.

https://books2read.com/r/B-A-EUTAB-TRUOC

BOOKS 2 READ

Connecting independent readers to independent writers.

Milton Keynes UK
Ingram Content Group UK Ltd.
UKHW010725190224
438095UK00001B/62

9 798215 418253